HAIL
MARY

HAIL MARY

FUNMI FETTO

MAGPIE
BOOKS

A Magpie Book

First published in the United Kingdom, Republic of Ireland and Australia
by Magpie Books, an imprint of Oneworld Publications Ltd, 2025

Copyright © Olufunmilola Fetto, 2025

The moral right of Olufunmilola Fetto to be identified as the Author of
this work has been asserted by her in accordance with the Copyright,
Designs, and Patents Act 1988

ISBN 978-0-86154-770-8
eISBN 978-0-86154-771-5

Printed and bound in Great Britain by Clays Ltd, Elcograf S.p.A

This book is a work of fiction. Names, characters, businesses,
organisations, places and events are either the product of the author's
imagination or are used fictitiously. Any resemblance to actual persons,
living or dead, events or locales is entirely coincidental.

Oneworld Publications Ltd
10 Bloomsbury Street
London WC1B 3SR
England

Stay up to date with the latest books,
special offers, and exclusive content from
Oneworld with our newsletter

Sign up on our website
oneworld-publications.com

<Dedication TK>

CONTENTS

SAMUEL 6:14 2

'And David danced before the LORD with all his might'

'**S**omebody shout Hallelooooooyeh! HALLELOOOOO-YEH! C'mon do you not know your God? Isn't this a time to celebrate? Psalm 100 tells us to *'make a joyful noise unto the Lord, serve the Lord with gladness, come into his presence with singing and into his courts with praise.'* So you need to get up on your feet and give the Lord A SHOUT OF PRAISE this Sunday morning! Brethren, it is time to worship the Lord. It's time to dance like David danced! Let's welcome the Praise and Worship team to the stage.'

Whenever Ifeoma came forward to address the congregation, she acted as if she was addressing a stadium of people. The church, optimistically built to seat a few hundred, housed on a good day, no more than sixty-five. Today, she wore a cheap pair of pink, plastic mules with an ill-fitting orange and brown Ankara dress that complemented her smooth light skin and highlighted the rolls around her thickened waist. Her 'word of encouragement', one she was tasked with presenting each service, was always delivered with an aggressively nasal American twang she'd acquired by religiously (but secretly) gorging on *Charlie's Angels* and watching *Different Strokes* on repeat. Her words bounced off the chipped monochromatic floors and dirty concrete walls of the colossal hall. Akin to the flat, painful din of the praise and worship team, it echoed beyond the vast room and into the compound from which it spilled its God-fearing gut onto the pot-holed streets of Agege. The members of Dunamis Power Ministries were convinced the deafening racket was a tool of deliverance for them and a weapon of salvation for unbelievers. Once it touched the hearts and minds of those whose lives were still dancing to the delights of the devil, they would finally see the light. Of course, Ifeoma was well aware that the devil was already doing his work much closer to home.

Recently, for the first time in years, Ifeoma didn't have to fake her enthusiasm during service. She actually felt genuine joy. And so, when the Praise and Worship team took to the stage and began to shout-sing, barking at the congregation to 'dance like David danced', she danced like David with all her girth, with all the enthusiasm she could muster. Sweat dripped freely down her heaving chest and her mouth ached from the fervency of her smile. In reality, her glee had nothing to do with being drunk on the Holy Spirit.

She was finally leaving. Of course she hadn't told anyone yet. Out of necessity, Ifeoma learned to master the art of keeping secrets. Besides, Pastor was the one who preached, 'When you are believing God for something precious, until it manifests, you have to keep it from evil eyes, from evil ears, lest it be taken away from you.' Once that 'something precious' manifests, he encouraged everyone to 'make the devil ashamed' by sharing the testimony with the church. 'Because after all, we are family,' he reminded the congregation.

Ifeoma had long lost touch with her own family. Her staunch Catholic mother and brothers were appalled that not only had she fallen for a man who came from generations of Muslims, she was determined to 'throw away her birthright for a Yoruba man. 'Tufiakwa!' her mother exclaimed in horror when Ifeoma initially, tentatively broached the possibility of marrying Pastor. 'These are *not* our people. And they are not good people. So, in the whole of Igbo land, there is no one you can find? Not one? What is wrong with Chibunna, Mrs Nwafor's son? Is he not good enough for you? Or Ikem

– that very handsome boy already on his way to becoming the best doctor in town? Or what about Emenike? What does it matter that he doesn't have the best face, at least we know who his people are. Why did you need to go outside and bring me news of this, this abomination of a man that is fifteen years your senior…' Her mother wept through her anger. 'Ifeoma, I've been raising you and your two brothers for how many years now since your father died and this is how you are going to do me?'

But Ifeoma was also angry. She didn't understand how her mother always had to always make everything about her. 'Mama, you got to choose your own husband, so why can't I choose mine?!'

Her mother responded by slapping her. 'You think that is how things are done? *Nwa m nwanyị*. If you do not listen to me, you will regret this decision for the rest of your life.'

Ifeoma had always been headstrong, 'stubborn like a boy', they said. (Over the years, Ifeoma would recall this and could almost taste the bitterness in her mouth as she mourned the woman she once was. How different would her life had been if she stayed 'stubborn, like a boy'.) She implored, begged, her mother and brothers to 'at least meet him' before deciding he wasn't right for her. They refused to and didn't attend the wedding. Her mother wrote to Ifeoma to inform her that she had been disowned by her and the family. *You are dead to us*, the letter said. Ifeoma was devastated. So, when Pastor said,

'After all, we are family', she understood how little meaning it carried.

When Ifeoma first met Pastor, almost twenty-five years ago, he was Lawal, the man who would become her husband. When his cousin died after refusing treatment on religious grounds for his failing liver, leaving behind a toddler and pregnant wife, Lawal began to question his own faith. 'What kind of God is this?' he said to her once. 'I'm sure if Taofik did this operation, he would still be alive today.'

He began to immerse himself in Christianity and the Bible, occasionally accompanying her to church, and eventually he raised his hand in response to the altar call. Initially, his conversion from Islam was a relief to Ifeoma. It seemed to quell his dark moments – Ifeoma had seen flashes of his temper during their courtship – and she was hopeful that his newfound zeal for Christ would prove her family wrong. And who knows, it might encourage a reconciliation, she hoped. But after having what he describes as his 'Damascus experience', Lawal reinvented himself as Pastor Luke and his fervency soon became terrifying; he would insist on 'staying in the spirit' for days where, besides preaching hellfire two-hour sermons at 5:00A.M. services every morning, he wouldn't speak with anyone and expected total silence in the house to 'avoid contamination.' Without warning, he also would insist she start a dry fast for thirty-six hours as a way to cleanse her 'from any fresh sins – known and unknown'.

The headaches she had from dehydration were blinding. Ifeoma, whether in public or in private, knew never to call him by his name especially not by Lawal – which he said 'died at the cross with his sins'. Even when they had sex – now, few and far between – she'd whisper 'Pastor' at his insistence. Early in their relationship, she would call him *'oko, mi'* as a term of endearment, a way of showing she was embracing all of him, including his native tongue which she still was not fluent in. On the rare occasions she referred to him as 'my husband' it no longer teemed with affection. It was simply a statement of fact.

She watched as Pastor walked – no, sprinted--up the stairs to the pulpit. To the naked eye, the pains in his chest, which he had privately complained of in recent weeks seems to have disappeared. But Ifeoma was unconvinced. He always preached that Christians 'giving their power to sickness' was evidence of 'immaturity' and that 'small faith will just give the devil a greater foothold in your life'. So, he would be loath to show his pain in public. Or it could be Pastor's 'sudden' recovery was because he now was flanked by Folashade, his busty, armour-bearer, who dutifully jiggled as she carried his gloriously frayed gigantic Bible and a bottle of (holy) iced water for him to drink during the service. It was a role usually occupied by a man; everyone knew this. Years ago, Folashade would have bothered her, but Ifeoma had long come to appreciate her husband's distractions – he had many over the years. It took his target off her back, if only fleetingly.

As the crowd hailed him, he smiled widely and drank in the adulation. He gave a sign for the worship team to leave the stage and opened his Bible, which Folashade had just placed reverently on the pulpit. An usher had moved the only functioning fan in the room so it was positioned to blow its cool breeze onto Pastor, keeping him comfortable, matte and as sweat free as possible. Everyone else had to quietly contend with the oppressive midday heat. But Ifeoma's mind was not preoccupied with the temperature. If her original plan didn't work soon, she would have a dilemma on her hands.

There was no way she could explain to Pastor that her name had been randomly selected for a green card without sounding deceitful. She began applying a few years ago after Kayode, the church's choirmaster who was studying to be a barrister, got his and left for Minnesota. She wasn't particularly interested in Minnesota; she just wanted to go to America. And while she and Kayode slept together on and off for the four years prior to his departure, Ifeoma's application to start a new life in America had nothing to do with her lover. Love didn't play a part in their arrangement. In fact, she purposely, consciously, denied herself the possibility.

An affair between an overweight, forty-four-year-old pastor's wife and an eligible twenty-five-year-old law student at church would be scandalous. He was likely to come out of it unscathed, but she would be called a witch and she'd be run out of town in disgrace. Or worse, certainly if Pastor had anything to do with it. And so Ifeoma knew the deal with Kayode. She accepted it for what it was and however long it lasted.

Ifeoma liked having a younger man. Kayode never shamed the evidence of her appetite, he relished her plumpness. He showed no restraint in his appreciation of it, hungrily exploring every crease and crevice of Ifeoma's fat body, indulging in things he could never ask of a nice born-again girl even after they got married. It was the first time in years that she felt desired, and it was just what she needed to reignite a sense of who she was before Pastor, before they had children. By her late teens she was aware that her light skin, full bust, fine features and the way her easy laugh juxtaposed with what men called 'stubbornness' – something they relished trying to break down – was a magnet. She was never short of suitors – though only a few were rewarded with her body – but she was always in control – even behind closed doors. It's what Pastor got to enjoy in the early days but eventually would punish her for. It was behaviour he described as lacking in 'godly restraint'. As the years went on, as her body grew, everything else of her shrunk. Giving Kayode the freedom to fulfill his lust – and yes, hers – without the fear of his chastisement felt like an easy exchange.

Every year that Ifeoma wasn't selected for her green card, was another year that her disappointment with life threatened to smother her. While the beatings from her husband became less frequent, there were still days when she fell into a place so dark she couldn't believe the omnipresent God could possibly exist there. On those days, she pretended to be sick so she didn't have to go into her job at the local bank. Eventually, she'd pick herself up and continue to apply in secret. She surprised herself – for many years, even the thought of being versatile with the truth, talk less of purposely hiding anything from her husband, filled her with a nauseating fear. Pastor was obsessed with 'the pursuit of truth' and was vociferous in his hatred for what he termed 'dangerous deceits'.

'Don't you know the devil is the father of lies?' he'd say. As much as she tried to bat it away, his words, like a tenacious mosquito, refused to leave her alone. It was a line that reverberated in her mind as Pastor often repeated it to their twin boys, Taiwo and Kehinde, over the years. He was always accusing them of one transgression or another; 'Who moved this newspaper from the table?' 'Is that the right way to say "Amen"?' 'I'm sure there were seven bottles of Coke here – who drank one? Tell the truth NOW and let the devil be ashamed!'

Despite his so-called 'pursuit of truth', regardless of the boys' answers, he would unemotionally, with faraway eyes, dish out his cruel punishments. Sometimes he would march them outside to the back of the house and leave them in the crushing heat for hours. He'd order them to kneel on the rough ground, keeping their arms above their heads while the sun singed their skin. Other times he would send them to bed without food and make them fast till 6:00P.M. the next day. Then there were the lashings. He gave those across the palms of their hands using his *koboko*. On one occasion it split Taiwo's palms open. One night after the boys had gone to bed, Ifeoma tried to discuss it with him, pleading with him to stop being so harsh with the children. Her words were tentative, her voice no higher than a whisper and she placed her hand on his arm hoping to soften him. He was displeased. 'Woman,' he retorted disdainfully, brushing her hand away. 'You call yourself a Christian?! Have you not read your Bible? If you spare the rod, you will spoil the child!' He paused and stared at her. 'And how dare you question me?' He made clear that there would be consequences – for both her and her children – if she were to try saving them from his wrath.

Over the years, she learnt to turn away, to steel her failing nerves, to convince herself – and later on, her sons – that it was for the best, telling them that, 'If we are patient and prayerful, things will change.' Back then, she actually believed it.

Her sons left home just before their eighteenth birthday; she went into their rooms one morning and discovered their clothes and shoes gone. Pastor ignored her desperate pleas to look for them.

'How will they cope? What will they find something to eat? Please, let us at least try to find them. Please,' she begged, until her cries became whispers. He responded impassively. 'No one chased them from this house. Just like the prodigal son, leave them to hunger for the food of pigs. When they are ready to repent, they can come home.'

When the boys finally got in touch almost two years later – a single letter addressed to her and signed in both their names but in what she recognized as Kehinde's handwriting – they revealed they had rejected the faith. Seeing as Pastor 'dished out his wickedness in the name of God', this was not a God they wanted to worship. But it was their words later that punctured her heart. 'But Mama, you are worse than him. You stood by and allowed it to happen.' These words would haunt her for the rest of her life. Pastor later discovered the letter, worn from her reading it over and over again. He dragged her into the kitchen by her braids and forced her to watch as he burned, over the stove, the only communication she had had with her sons. He then banned her from corresponding with them. 'If thy right eye offends thee,' he said as the paper disintegrated into ash, 'pluck it out, and cast it from thee: for it is profitable for thee that one of thy members should perish, and not that thy whole body should be cast into hell...' He ran his slim thumb across the palms of his hands, wiping away the only remnants of his sons. 'If they want to live Godless lives and perish, leave them to perish.'

After the letter, the house began to feel like a blacked-out room with no windows and no doors, a world where the light existed somewhere in the distance. It was then she finally let go of her faith.

Shortly thereafter, she began her affair with Kayode.

They met after he moved into a small tenement house nearby and joined their church. One Sunday, they caught each other's eye. She knew what the look meant but she had to be sure. It was dangerous. And he was young enough to be her son. He was not particularly tall – in her heels Ifeoma was taller than him – but he was sturdy, had strong mature features and the beautiful dark skin she initially fell for when Pastor was Lawal. 'What a decent young man,' Pastor would say of Kayode, after inviting him and his small, dull girlfriend – who was only around sporadically as she was studying medicine in Ibadan – to lunch with them after service one day months after their entanglement began. Kayode was careful not to exchange many words with Ifeoma, except to prostrate every time he greeted her, and call her 'Ma'. She bristled inwardly – it reminded her of their age difference. But his behaviour would ensure no one suspected a thing. Soon Pastor began asking Kayode to drop Ifeoma home from church on the days their driver Samson wasn't around.

She didn't know Kayode was applying for a green card; there were limits to their relationship and they did not discuss such things. But she suspected he was keen to explore what life offered beyond his life in Mushin and his boring fiancée-to-be, who, in the end, he left.

Ifeoma would love to leave Pastor, too. It had crossed her mind to get away in secret, but she sensed he would somehow find a way to bring her back and punish her for it. So, if her initial plan didn't work, she reasoned, she would just have to find a strategic way to tell him about her own green card, which had finally arrived in the mail earlier in the week after years of applying. She couldn't sound too happy, too proud, too celebratory, too…anything. She needed to emphasize how this opportunity would benefit him. Maybe she would explain how it would enable her to work and send money back to him; he understood the language of foreign currency. It could help to buy more land to build the big, bigger, biggest church for all the other local pastors to envy. He could then join her in America, and he could open a branch abroad, the beginning of his international ministry! Of course this would all be the last resort. Only if her original plan didn't work.

As Ifeoma took her seat at church waiting for her husband to start preaching, her left foot began tapping of its own accord. It always did when she was anxious. Ifeoma shifted in her seat, as she felt a pain. She bit down on her lip to stop herself from crying out. She could still feel the pinch of the three-day old welts from Pastor's belt. They decorated the back of her thick thighs.

'Have you fully given your life to Christ,' Pastor bellowed out from the pulpit. 'Some of you here,' he pointed a finger, his eyes sweeping, accusatory, across the congregation, 'are fornicating. You know who you are!' Ifeoma huffed inwardly at the hypocrisy of his condemnation. She had begun secretly sleeping with Pastor long before they were married, while they were attending another church. At the time, Ifeoma burned with shame thinking of all the things they did. It was not becoming of a well brought up Catholic. There were things he still made her do. Except now, he did so in retribution.

Pastor wasn't always violent. So said his aunt with whom he grew up. She tells of a once-affable and even kind human being. Admittedly, Ifeoma did see glimmers of that man when they first began dating. But Lawal was never someone she would have described as gentle; there was an element of his roughness, from the sound of his voice to the stubble on his face to the flash of danger in his eyes, that excited her. At the time, it didn't occur to her that the persistent but simultaneously transient unease she felt was something to be afraid of. He always countered his dominating nature with a lavish amount of attention towards her. She was flattered by how possessive he was of her; his blatant, bold expression of how much he desired her was something she had never really known with other men. Lawal was older, more experienced and a world away from the fumbling boys she had messed around with back home in Enugu. He told her he was on a mission to conquer her, and he did exactly that. Lawal was a drug, and she was thoroughly addicted.

'But,' Aunty once said to Ifeoma, 'war can do terrible things to a man.' He had joined the army as a teenager and when he returned four years later, 'He was', recalls Aunty, 'the same but…different. Sometimes, I did not recognize him.' Ifeoma spent the first few years of her marriage thinking the same. There were moments she didn't recognize the man she married. There was something of a paradox where his love for her and his fury with her were concerned. They seemed equally intense. Perhaps it is why initially she justified the abuse and was too ashamed to speak to anyone about it. Besides, she rarely saw her friends. Pastor didn't like them or think they were good for her. When she spoke to God and didn't get an answer, she turned to Aunty. Her house was one of the few places she could go without being questioned too much. It was Aunty who invited her around, as a matter of urgency prior to their wedding, so she could learn how to cook Pastor's favourite Yoruba dishes. On the first day, Aunty explained why these lessons were so important. 'If you don't feed your husband, somebody else will feed him for you,' she said knowingly. 'You don't want a husband that has to go outside to be satisfied.'

Ten years into their marriage, after a particularly aggressive altercation that left her ribs bruised, her ears ringing and her voice hoarse from screaming in pain as well as in anger, Ifeoma finally decided, in her desperation, to speak to Aunty. She recounted a few of the many incidents involving her nephew: there was the hot plate of rice he threw at her because he preferred the stew to be on the side and not on top; there were the women who would call the house, sometimes late at night, and once when she confronted him, he chased her around the house with his belt. She was pregnant at the time and miscarried. On the drive back from dropping the twins off at boarding school, Lawal accused her of speaking out of turn in front of the principal. He asked the driver to stop the car, pushed her out, shut the door and commanded the driver to keep moving. With no money on her person for a taxi or even water, she had to walk the rest of the journey home – just over six miles – in the staggering heat.

Aunty sighed, but as she spoke, her face was unmoved. 'My dear, you have to try to understand Yoruba men. They need patience. Why don't you start by trying your best to please him? Do what he wants, don't make him angry, don't talk too much and everything will be okay,' she advised in her broken English. 'And,' she added with a smile, scrutinizing Ifeoma's face and exposed arms, 'at least you can be thankful you have the beautiful kind of skin that doesn't mark easily.'

When Ifeoma attended Aunty's funeral a few years later, she didn't shed a tear.

But Ifeoma had seen the warning signs early in her and Lawal's relationship and was angry at herself for not heeding them. While they were courting, Lawal had invited her to a party at the Victoria Palace Hotel with some of his friends. Lawal was unusually quiet on the way home. It was late; she was naive, and she interpreted his reserve for tiredness. As soon as they walked through the front door into the living area, he turned and slapped her, pushing her onto the sofa in his small dark apartment and grabbed her hair, keys still in hand. He did enjoy a little bit of rough play, something she was slowly trying to get used to but this time she was even more unsure that she liked it.

'So, you, this useless Igbo girl,' he said, his voice hoarser than usual but still calm. 'You want to come and embarrass me in this town? Eh?'

Ifeoma was bewildered. 'What are you talking about? What have I done?'

There was a bitter edge to his laugh. 'You don't know what you did? You think I didn't see the way you were looking at Gbenga? Opening your mouth with all your teeth like you wanted him to put his thing in it?'

Ifeoma's eyes widened at the accusation and her words failed her. Somewhere deep down, she prayed he would start laughing, telling her it was a joke, and he was just testing her, playing one of his curious games. But he didn't. Instead, he stared at her face and began grabbing parts of her body with his free hand, parts she had given him permission to touch before, but not now, not tonight, not like this. 'Is this what you were thinking of? Is this what you wanted from Gbenga?' Ifeoma's mind raced as she tried to recall her scant interactions with Gbenga at the party. He had only asked her – and many of the other women at their table – what they wanted to drink. She could remember no other conversation with Gbenga because she hadn't had any.

Ifeoma tried to move from under Lawal, his bulky knee pinning her down; escape was futile. She found herself look-ing towards the thick green, printed gabardine curtains that were a little too big for the window, the brownish discolour-ation on the peeling ceiling, the heavy wooden door... Save me, she thought. Save me.

The sudden realization of just how disempowered she was, brought on a fresh, elevated wave of fear and Ifeoma began to sob. 'Lawal please, please stop, what have I done? What did I do wrong? I wasn't flirting with anyone; I wasn't looking at anyone... Please, I'm begging you... please...stop this. I just want to go home.' Her nose began to stream in harmony with her tears. 'Please let me get up. I don't know what I've done.'

He suddenly stopped. But Ifeoma couldn't stop sobbing. She could smell herself on his left hand as he cupped her face and used the cuff from his right sleeve to clean her nose. And then, with the wet cuff began to wipe the bright pink lipstick from her mouth with such brute force her lips bled. Finally, he lifted his weight off her and began walking towards the door. Without turning around, keys jingling in his hands, he said 'When you finish crying your *ye ye* tears, come outside and I'll drop you home.'

For months after, she refused to see him. He came to the Ikeja apartment she shared with an old school friend from Enugu; she refused to open the door for him, so he stood outside her door begging for her forgiveness. He brought her gifts. He sent letters. In them, he told her how much he loved her, that she was the only one for him, that he wanted her to be his wife, that he hadn't slept for months, that he missed her , that he had lost his appetite, that he couldn't stop thinking about her, that he was sorry, that he had lost his mind with jealousy, that the drink did it, that it would never happen again. Ifeoma often wondered how different her life would have been, who she would have been, if she had held on to her resolve to never see him again. Instead, what she did then was to leverage her moment. It was an opportunity to address another issue that had been a sore point very early on in their relationship. Yes, with her family, but if she was being honest with herself, marrying a Yoruba man was one thing. Marry a Muslim man? This was never something that truly sat well with her. What would happen down the line? Would he suddenly decide to take his faith more seriously? Would she have to start covering her head? Would she have to give up work? Would she have to give up her rights as a woman? Would he want to take an extra wife? Or two? Or more? And expect her to turn a blind eye to it? She had heard too many horror stories from born-again women that grew up in polygamous homes. She gave him an ultimatum: 'Yes, I know you are not a practising Muslim, but that is not the point. I cannot and will not marry a non-Christian,' she said, relishing her newfound power. 'The book of Amos asks, "How can two walk together unless they are agreed?" A Muslim and a Christian are not agreed. I don't want to be unequally yoked with my husband.'

He responded, 'Ifeoma, all I know is this. I want you to be my wife. And so I will do whatever it takes.' Her heart leapt and she knew at that moment, her will, which had already been worn down to the bones, was completely broken. When she finally opened her bedroom door to face him, she said with a smile. 'Well, if you want to marry me, then you know what to do.' She has spent the last twenty-five years wishing she had kept the door – and her mouth – shut.

After the church service, Ifeoma remained seated as the members of the congregation came to greet her, as they always did. Her husband had already begun leaving for the church office at the other end of the compound, as he did every Sunday. Folashade, who had taken it upon herself to ensure Pastor's lunch – usually *iyan* with *efo riro* and assorted meats, which Ifeoma had made earlier in the morning and kept in a cooler – was ready to serve in fifteen minutes. It was a heavy meal, made to sustain him in the many hours after service he spent conducting counselling sessions with members of the congregation. Or so he said. She learnt for the sake of peace to react with nothing more than a smile and a nod. As she fake-smiled with the crowd of people greeting her with 'First Lady', she was well aware that they would much rather be up close and personal with Pastor. The hem of his garment was much more powerful than hers could ever be. After wading through the crowd, their driver Samson approached her to tell her the car was ready to take her home. Ifeoma was grateful not to have the fortnightly women's meeting after church today. It was where she would teach the women – married and single – how to be a submissive wife, how to keep quiet when your husband was angry, how, as a woman, they should be the peacekeeper, how to never withhold sex from him, how to remember that he was the head of the house and how the woman's role was to support the man in that very pressurized position. A woman was, as Pastor once told her, like Eve – 'merely ribs'. Of course, she no longer believed this. Everything she had become is everything he had forced her to become, everything she never was, everything she came to hate.

Ifeoma entered the car and immediately smelt a heavy floral perfume. It wasn't hers. It was pointless asking Samson anything. He was far too loyal to Pastor who came second only to God for him. She adjusted herself across the back seats to make her welts more comfortable.

'Samson, she asked, as they drove out of the compound, 'Did you buy the powder I asked you to buy? We are still seeing those things running around the kitchen'.

'Yes, Ma,' he replied, I bought the strongest one, like the one you asked for.'

'Okay, thank you. Make sure you don't mention it to Pastor. You know he does not like to hear those things.'

'Yes, Ma'.

When they arrived at the house, Samson carried Ifeoma's bags inside and headed back to the church to wait for Pastor.

Their house girl was away for a week visiting relatives in her village which meant Ifeoma would be alone for a few hours until Pastor's arrival, which she loved. She went into her bedroom, took a shower and changed into her house clothes. She took out a VHS recording with multiple epi-sodes of *Different Strokes* and began watching while drinking a bowl of *gari* and *epa*. It was the only time she could watch what he would consider 'secular' – a word he associated with anything he deemed 'the works of the devil.' After an hour, she switched off, took the VHS back to her room, hid it behind the wardrobe and headed to the kitchen to cook. Her husband was usually back home by around 7:00P.M at which time he expected to be served dinner. Today she made a fresh tilapia stew which she would serve with rice and fried plantain. She stirred a few maggi cubes into the pot and then sprinkled in a little of the white powder Samson had picked up for her. For the past three weeks, she had been adding ant killer to Pastor's food. Not enough for him to taste it, of course. But enough to do slow harm. It had not been having the effect she expected, however. At least, not quickly enough. So, she asked Samson to pick up something much stronger to kill rodents. She stirred again and gingerly placed the lid on the simmering pot.

Outside, she heard the car race into the compound, its wheels crackling over the grit of the grounds. Her heart leapt into her mouth. She looked at the giant clock in the dining room. It was only 5:45P.M. Lawal was early.

But it was Samson's voice she heard at once. 'Madam! Madam! First Lady!'

She rushed outside to see their panicked driver running to the door. She didn't see Lawal. 'Samson! Ah, ah! Why are you shouting like this? What is the problem?'

'It's Pastor! You have to come now. He has collapsed, we took him to the hospital, you have to come now. Now, now! You have to come. Now! First Lady, they say it could be organ failure! This is serious. O! Ah, God help us! Please Ma, you have to come now, now, now!' Samson looked shaken and close to tears.

Ifeoma's hand flew dramatically to her chest. 'Let me quickly get my shoes and my Bible'. She hurried back into her room and closed the door. She lifted up her mattress and pulled out the approval letter for her green card. And Ifeoma began to dance. She danced and she danced and she danced. Just like David danced.

UNSPOKEN

Seven P.M. When James presented her with the ring – standing, not kneeling, his face close to hers – she smiled. She was surprised. Not because she didn't know it was coming, but because she didn't know it would be here, today, in the cozy, old-money Pimlico drawing room of Portia, one of his oldest friends, surrounded by many more of his friends from home, most of whom Amaka, at best, tolerated. But as the deafening crescendo of excitement reverberated around the room, she kept the smile on her face. She smiled wider still as they all raised their glasses to James's proclamation that this was '*The beginning of forever.*' By now they had all risen from their seats, all jabbering and cheering but not in unison... She could barely hear herself speak. But she continued to smile. So much so that no one noticed that she didn't actually utter the word 'yes'. James threw his arms around her waist, drew her in for a kiss and she obliged. That was all the 'yes' he and everyone in the room needed. Through the raucous chatter and applause, no one heard the nervous laughter escaping her lips, punching holes through her bewildered smile.

Eleven-thirty P.M. Now in the privacy of her own walls, in a tiny West London flat where she insisted on living alone, Amaka no longer smiled. As she poured herself some brandy neat, she stared blankly at the ring, a slim, rose-gold band, at its centre, a raised cluster of antique diamonds. It once belonged to James's French great-grandmother, and he'd had it adjusted for her benefit. Her own 'very African hands', which her secondary-school art teacher kindly offered as the reason for Amaka's ineptitude at the 'delicate art of pottery', were bigger than those of its petite former owner. Stretching out her left hand, she analyzed her fourth finger as if it belonged to someone else. She mulled over the repercussions of the ring. What did '*the beginning of forever*' mean? Commitment? How much was required? Would she have to share *everything*? Some doors had been intentionally, actively kept shut. Then there was the question of children. How *whole* do you need to be to justify bringing other humans into the world? The only blueprint she knew was not one she wanted to follow. And then there was the more immediate issue of church. James mentioned that premarital sessions with a reverend were a 'healthy way to unpack any issues' before marriage. He tried to sound breezy, but Amaka knew what he was saying. She said nothing. She was not ready to discuss her 'issues' with anyone, not a therapist, not James and not even a man of the cloth. She did not believe in God. Certainly not after 'The Incident'. She couldn't help the dry laugh that escaped through her lips. Even at the time, when the officials described what happened as such, she couldn't help internally grimacing, thinking the term hackneyed and unimaginative.

Amaka's father appeared infrequently throughout her childhood. And when he did, it was always within a strangely clandestine atmosphere. Once, out of the blue, an angry stranger with a loud voice called her mother from Nigeria. It was then Amaka discovered that her father had his *real* family living with him in Lagos: a wife and four children, who were damned if they were going to acknowledge the 'bastards' that had resulted from an affair with a 'low-class Jezebel' in the UK.

After The Incident, her father came to London. The authorities assumed he was coming to take responsibility for his children. He left after three days and Amaka and Joseph were left with professional foster parents. George and Sally Whitting, a lower-middle-class couple, so nondescript they seemed to blend into each other, lived out in Earl Soham, a small, wholly white-populated village in East Anglia. It was a bucolic world away from the urban surroundings of their brutalist council flat in South London. Amaka and her brother were told they were very 'lucky', that they were to be 'grateful' they had not been placed in care homes or split up, because even twins didn't always find families willing to take them both in. 'And,' continued their stout, poker-faced case worker, 'think of this as an incredible chance for a new start, a wonderful opportunity to be exposed to things' that Amaka and Joseph had never experienced in London. Things like horse-riding lessons, playing games of croquet on immaculate lawns, going for long walks in muddy fields, breathing in air unencumbered by city smog, avoiding nettles while picking wild blackberries to make jam with. 'That's if you haven't eaten most of them before you get home...' she'd mused. Amaka had to concede; it *was* different to anything she had known.

Except the racism. That was still familiar, just dressed up differently. Back then, despite not quite having the language for it, she recognized the multifarious ways in which it presented itself. They were stared at on the streets of Debenham, on the beach in Aldeburgh, in the shops of Framlingham. At school, she invited either (innocent?) curiosity ('Why does your hair feel so –' the blonde girl had wrinkled her snub nose in confusion as she searched for the right word '– so *fat* and woolly?') or outright derision ('Where's your Um Bongo? Isn't that what you drink in the Congo?'– followed by the screeching sounds of a monkey). It was pointless trying to explain that her heritage was Nigerian, not Congolese. That she was born in St Thomas' Hospital just by Westminster Bridge in the centre of London. That she'd never been to Congo, or Africa or drunk Um Bongo – her mother took umbrage at the jungle-themed advert, kissing her teeth whenever it was on. But she kept quiet. She wasn't special; the racism wasn't just directed at her. Misa, the only person of Asian descent in their school, was regularly taunted – it was either Slitty-Eye Misa or, if they had time, a rendition of the theme tune from the popular children's show, *The Wide Awake Club*, ('We're wide awake! It's good to know you're ready and you're wide awake!) With the exception of the odd banana that would randomly appear in his bag, Joseph, on the other hand, seemed to fare much better. His easy, charming manner countered her quiet awkwardness. Girls swarmed him. Amaka suspected this was less to do with her brother's charm and everything to do with country-bumpkin teens rebelling against their parents. Having a black boyfriend was forbidden fruit, their way of living on the edge. Joseph was also popular with the boys; the combination of his bulk and agility made him a natural rugby player. If you helped to bring in The Cup, no one cared if you were Black.

Amaka and Joseph never discussed The Incident. They had the obligatory counselling sessions – *separate* counselling sessions – which they also never discussed. After a number of years, Amaka, old enough and strong enough not to have her will be overridden, stopped seeing the various therapists assigned to her. She couldn't see the point of confiding in someone who was *paid* to listen. Also, surely it was dull for them? She barely spoke and never cried. It all seemed like a terrible waste of everyone's time. One summer, Joseph packed his bags to be with an (older) Italian woman he had met on an international rugby trip the year before. Except he never really came back. Initially, Amaka saw him once a year – usually at the stilted 'family' Christmas dinners with the Whittings that nobody enjoyed but everyone felt duty bound to attend. Soon enough, even that tailed off. Last she heard from her brother, he had broken up with Alissia and was moving to LA with some other love interest to pursue a career as a scriptwriter. He became more elusive and Amaka gave up trying to pin him down. On the rare occasions he got in touch, Amaka felt privileged (how nice that he thought of her). But she also felt uncomfortable. His calls were an unwanted reminder of her past, *their* past. She suspected, based on how overly cheery, ambiguous and brief his calls were, that Joseph felt the same.

Hence, he had long cut ties with George and Sallie. Amaka on the other hand still felt a gnawing sense of loyalty to the couple, even when their once pitiful and patient eyes long became passive. She couldn't blame them. She was like a block of ice that inexplicably hardened –not melted – under the warmth of the sun. Amaka didn't risk opening up. Not for fear of melting but for the terror of shattering into tiny, painful, shards of glass. And who would pick them up? On the rare days they were all at home together, they began to avoid the discomfort of each other's company. When the Whittings' *real* daughter's marriage began to crumble and the house became a refuge for her and her two young children, Amaka didn't need anyone to ask her to leave.

One-thirty A.M. Amaka opened her side drawer and looked at the letters that had accumulated over time. Most were unopened. *'Amaka Ejiofor'* was scrawled in the same swirly but brusque handwriting, the *k* in her name written like an *r* with a long but disjointed sidebar. The most recent arrival was different. Similar envelope, familiar postmark, but this time she had to sign for it. Many years ago, she made the mistake of opening the very first letter and it was such a shock. Hence, the consequent letters that arrived every nine to twelve months since were left sealed. She considered burning them, but it was easier to stuff them in a drawer which she closed, firmly, belligerently, secretly, wishing the process would turn them to ash. She stared at the latest letter, resentful that, once again, she had been forced into a situation she was unable to control. James was aware of her past – no details, just the headlines – but nevertheless she kept all the letters from him. He believed in everything being aired 'like laundry', whereas Amaka was satisfied with the silence of things left unspoken. She would laugh wryly when he complained at her unrivalled ability to bury her emotions. Her response was always that he should be grateful – a dysfunctional case study like her would keep his brain busy well into his twilight years. Now she wasn't so sure.

Three A.M. The half bottle of brandy was empty and Amaka's mind increasingly began drifting in and out of the present. Nothing in the day leading up to The Incident gave any hint of things to come. As always, she let herself and her brother into the flat after school let out. It was winter – she clearly remembers her numb fingers having difficulty positioning the key in the lock. Their mother was in bed. In a few hours, she would start getting ready. By then, Amaka would have already prepared a meal for both her and her brother to eat – be it white rice and mixed vegetables to go with a traditional meat stew she would have cooked during the weekend or potatoes she cut and fried to eat with chicken pies and freshly made baked beans. It had been this way for as long as Amaka could remember. By the time she was eleven, she was so adept in the kitchen her mother would joke that she was ready to become someone's wife. She remembers it being a

Friday because, although Joseph was already in front of the television in his full uniform, when their mother saw him she didn't shout at him to go and change. It was customary for her mother to ask them both how their day was, what they had learnt, even if she didn't pay much attention to their responses. She would always tell them that they had to work hard at school. 'Education is the best way to make it in life,' she'd say. Even then, Amaka thought it was funny their mother couldn't see the irony in what she was saying. From a distance, Amaka would watch the ritual of her mother getting ready, usually with a glass of something in her hand. It was the only time the bedroom door was left wide open.

At thirty-eight, although her *joie de vivre* had faded somewhat by the life she led, traces of Amaka's mother's beauty remained. She was still very elegant. She never wore black – her underwear was always white, not cream or ivory or off-white but a pure-as-the-driven-snow white. On her neck and chest, she squirted Robert Piguet's *Fracas*. She had done so ever since she was first given the expensive scent as a gift. She did this even when *Charlie* was the fashionable perfume of the time because, 'men don't remember women who smell like every woman'. Amaka was always intrigued by the five, white polystyrene heads topped with synthetic wigs that lined her dressing table. (In the years that followed, Amaka had a recurrent dream that featured each of these heads soaked in blood.) That evening, as always, their mother powdered her face, filled out her eyebrows with black kohl and put on a freshly ironed outfit. The outfit of choice that night was a close-fitting, white wraparound blouse and a pair of white thigh-hugging bell bottoms. She added a pair of emerald-green earrings and red patent heels with a see-through PVC platform. Around her neck, hung the small gold sovereign she never took off. (It now hangs around Amaka's neck.) She sat back down and reached for one of the wigs. Today it was the short, light brown bob with a heavy fringe. After placing it over her cornrows and running her fingers through the strands, she applied a bright red gloss, smacked her lips together and slipped the lipstick tube into her handbag. As if on cue, a car beeped outside. 'Okay,' she said cheerily as Amaka trailed her towards the front door, 'I'll see you later. Make sure you don't open the door for any-body. And don't pick up the phone if it rings… Joseph!' she shouted in the direction of the TV. 'Make sure you don't give your sister problems!' Amaka spent the evening reading; she was going through her S.E Hinton phase and was engrossed with *Rumble Fish*. Joseph watched television to his heart's delight. He eventually fell asleep by the screen, and she had to wake him to get to bed. After changing into her pyjamas, she made her way to her own bed and continued reading until sleep took her.

Amaka was awakened by the sound of her mother's shrill, slightly drunk giggle and the front door slamming behind her. There was another voice – a man's voice. Amaka was used to this. It didn't happen often but sometimes the men – polite, well dressed, well spoken – would sheepishly slip away when the day broke, hoping not to be seen. Over the years, her mother breezily introduced her and Joseph to a roster of men, calling each of them 'her friend'. Bayo (good-looking, stale breath). Nick (tall, silver hair, kind smile). Julian (small ears, terrible shoes, laughed a lot). Mo (long forehead, expensive smelling). Charles (smoked cigars, thick dark eyebrows, had his arm permanently glued to their mother's waist, brought gifts). No one needed to tell her what her mother did for a living. Was it official? Amaka couldn't be sure. All she knew was that her mother had long stopped cleaning offices early in the morning, there were men, and there was an ever-growing stash of cash under her mother's mattress. Lots and lots of cash. Unlike Joseph, who could sleep through an earthquake, some of Amaka's nights were spent with cotton wool stuffed in her ears and her head under her pillow just to blot out the intimate noises coming from their mother's room.

Later that morning, Amaka and Joseph were having their breakfast. The crackle of Rice Krispies popped in her ears, her brother's eyes, once again, glued to the television. She could hear her mother and her male friend in the bedroom. The conversation was fraught. And loud. 'But I don't understand. I told you. *I* will look after you, you don't have to do this anymore… I don't want you to keep doing this. Is it about money? I'll give you money. Why the fuck can't you just stop?' Amaka recognized Nick's exasperated voice. A 'friend' who had recently become more than a client. Her mother sounded enraged. 'No, no, no, no, Nick, YOU stop. How many times are we going to have this? I told you I don't need any man to look after me. You knew what you were getting into. I can make my own way. Why do I need your money? What, so that in the end you can oppress me with it?' Amaka wasn't sure what Nick said in response, the snap, crackle and pop of the Rice Krispies drowned out his words, but she did hear her mother's bitter laugh. 'You think you're the first man to tell me that? So, I should wait while you try to leave your wife? You think I'm stupid?'. Back and forth it went until, her appetite long gone, Amaka could no longer pretend to eat. Her eyes met Joseph's. He nervously turned away and increased the TV volume. The argument got louder and more intense, her mother now telling Nick in no uncertain terms to leave. In quick succession, thuds were followed by a crashing sound and then a scream. A terrifying, animalistic scream. Amaka felt her insides curdle. She knocked over her bowl of cereal as she and her brother made their way towards their mother's room, her bare feet covered in milk and cereal. 'Mummy?' She opened the door in time to see Nick smashing an iron into her mother's head for the final time as she lay stiff on the floor. Amaka could barely make out her face; it was already drenched in blood. Nick's cotton trousers, his bare chest, his hands, even his mouth were all splashed a dark, rich red. As was her mother's white underwear. He didn't drop the iron. He began to weep. Amaka doesn't remember where Joseph stood. She doesn't remember who called the police. She remembers the childish, canned laughter reverberating from the overly loud TV and the sticky feel of milk-soaked cereal under her feet.

Seven A.M. Amaka woke up with a start. She felt rotten and was grateful it was a Saturday. She showered and changed into an old T-shirt and jeans. '*This is the beginning of forever*' echoed in her aching head. She pulled out the drawer with force and tipped all the letters out. Averting her eyes, she stuffed them into a carrier bag. She placed the drawer back in its place and put on her trainers. It was then she realized the 'signed for' letter was still sitting on her side table. She took a deep breath. *This is the beginning of forever*, she thought as she began to rip it open. '*I can do this, I can do this, I can do this*,' she repeatedly whispered. As she absorbed its contents, Amaka still didn't quite understand why Nick's wife carried the guilt of her husband murdering his prostitute lover. Or why, over the years she wrote to her. Did she expect Amaka to relieve her of the burden? Did she think by informing Amaka about Nick's rapidly deteriorating brain tumour it would make everything better? *By the time you receive this, he will most likely be dead*, wrote

Elizabeth. She left her telephone number...*if ever you want to talk...*

She rang James. 'I'm so sorry... We can't get married... I can't get married... Yes, I'm serious... No, you haven't done anything wrong... I just need to deal with my stuff... Yeah, finally... No, you don't understand, there's no *we* in this. There's *me*. Just me. I need to do this alone...'. Amaka crumpled the final letter. Adding it to the bag with the hope that this would be the last, she made her way to the local council tip. She wondered what Joseph was doing. Had he received letters? She would never know. 'We don't talk about The Incident, remember?' he had smiled sadly when she once dared, tentatively, to approach the subject. That was the closest they had come to acknowledging its existence. After throwing the bag of letters into the tip, she stretched out her ring free hands. On the way home Amaka popped into the supermarket to pick up some milk. For coffee. Nothing else. Ever since 'The Incident', she had never been able to face another bowl of cereal.

HAIL MARY

It's Mother's Day again. And so today, Riliwa, standing in her drab, box room, consciously kept the radio off. There was something unnerving listening to the endless drizzle of syrupy proclamations. She has no interest in hearing trite song requests lauding mothers or motherhood. The root cause of Riliwa's consternation was a realization that no one ever admits to having an ugly mother. No one. 'How is that possible?' she said to herself aloud. All her life, she herself knew lots of ugly mothers. There were the mother's society deemed aesthetically ugly, like those with facial features that were thrown together like awkward strangers that spoke different languages. There were those who were big, not big like those young women – not her, she purposely made herself invisible – that men would cat call on the streets of Peckham, shamelessly eyeing their bodies, praising it for its Coca-Cola bottle shape. No, these were ones who were big, fat, where the fat filled like rolls around their necks, filled the creases of their arms, around their ankles... It was a sluggish fat that was distributed in a way that left its victim totally out of proportion. There were those who felt no embarrassment plucking at the excessive thickened black hair around their chin as they gossiped at the back of their tenement yard back home in Nigeria. Or those obsessively applying lightening creams to erase evidence of the dark shade they were born with, only to discover that the gossamer-thin sheath beneath was too fragile against the blaze of the sun. And so it quickly became a patchwork of grotesquely discoloured skin that only served to spotlight the blackness they tried to erase. Then there were those like her. On the surface she didn't resemble any of those ugly women but of course, she knew she was an ugly mother. Even if it was in pursuit of a so-called better life, only ugly mothers abandon their children; society deems her ugly.

The doorbell went. Riliwa froze. Fear had become so steeped in her everyday living that her bones felt permanently stiff, her shoulders ever raised. But she had learnt to live with the ache so that most days she even forgot it was there. The bell went again. It was a Sunday morning, but she didn't assume it was safe. She could see the front of the house from her small window, but she didn't dare move the curtains, just in case. Her breath of relief only came when she could hear a voice in the hallway, one speaking Arabic to someone else on the phone and then another voice followed by the calm closing of the front door. The house had been so still she had forgotten that not everyone would have gone to church or work. She opened her bedroom door to see Mustafa speaking with his male friend as they made their way downstairs to his room.

'*Salaam Alaikum*,' he said, slightly sheepishly when he saw her; his young guest nodded his greeting to her.

'*Salaam Alaikum*,' she responded without smiling. Ever since Mustafa discovered she had also come from a Muslim home – of course she herself had never really been a practising or believing Muslim – it formed an unspoken connection. As she made her way into the kitchen, she felt riddled with guilt at her hypocrisy. She couldn't help but think how he would absolutely not get away with that behaviour back home in his country. She had never been to Algeria, but as a fellow African, she knew enough about their continent that any sign of homosexuality, whether tacit or explicit, would be openly condemned. Sometimes violently. While of course she could never justify that – they are human beings like everyone else, she knew – but there was something about it that didn't sit well with her. In normal circumstances, their social circles would never cross. But this was London and London was a leveller. They lived in a large but derelict and unkempt house in an unfashionable part of East London filled with other African immigrants – from Nigeria, Togo, Uganda, Congo, Algeria. Immigrants who, just like her, while repulsed by the rodents, cockroaches and damp that faithfully lived amongst them in the house, were grateful for a landlord that asked no questions, the cheap rent, and fellow occupants who all minded their own business. They were all runaways, hiding from something or someone or somewhere.

After her breakfast, a bland but filling bowl of cornflakes from a no-name brand, Riliwa began to get ready to head to Mary's to call her mother back home. Lately it hadn't been as regular as she would have liked it. It was expensive, but also, she couldn't bite her lip enough to pretend that everything was 'fine', that living in London wasn't brutal to foreigners, that despite juggling two menial jobs, she had enough to eat, that her loneliness wasn't crippling, that there weren't days she thought of the son she'd left behind and wept till she was raw. And so, she would write letters for her brother to translate to their mother. It was the easiest way to communicate without revealing too much. When she did call, she would simply pick up where she left off the last time, apologizing for the lack of communication. 'Ah, Mama you know London is busy,' she would say breezily, and carry on the charade. If only to allay the unfounded suspicion that her mother may have that her daughter had become a stalwart in the British sex industry, which as far as her mother was concerned was how every African girl ended up if she wasn't careful. Riliwa often recalls and rues the day a few years ago she prepared to leave home. Her mother's contempt for the western world had been inflamed by speaking with Mrs Kudu - their neighbor, a notorious gossip who had barely left their town in Osun state. She told Riliwa's mother that London was a place of debauchery and everything that Allah stood against. She said it was where girls from good families are influenced and encouraged to sleep with white men for money so that they can pretend to everyone back home that they are prospering.

'What type of useless place is this London?' Mrs Momodu disapprovingly eyed up the bottle-green pencil skirt her daughter was folding into the light-brown leatherette suitcase in the centre of their cramped living room floor. She was now muttering her disgust at a TV programme that showed 'half naked women dancing like prostitutes'.

Riliwa now raised her voice, exasperated at this daily diatribe that had begun two months ago when she told her mother she was going to England. 'Mama, *ejo. Tori olorun e ma bere leni.* Please don't start. Not today. Please. Anyway, that *Soul Train* show you are talking about is not even from London. I've told you before. It's American.'

Mrs Momodu widened her eyes dramatically and made a face. 'So, you are now correcting me? Because you are going to London, you are now a big madam correcting me, *abi*?'

'Mama, why are you behaving like this? How am I correcting you? I was just telling you that the show is from America. I'm going to London; I'm not going to America.' Riliwa noted her mother's demeanour change once again. Her lips twisted to the side, and she clasped her hands together, rubbing her left thumb over the right. This meant, from what she knew of her mother, that Mrs Momodu had taken the last sentence as an affront. Riliwa winced inwardly, annoyed at herself at rising, once again, to her mother's complaints. She looked back down scanning the chaos of clothes, shoes and miscellaneous items scattered around the floor. Her brow furrowed trying to establish what next to pack into the large case. Mrs Momodu, feigning sarcastic defeat, slapped the back of her hand into the palm of the other. 'Okay, I see I can't even talk or ask questions in my own house without my own daughter telling me my mouth is stinking.'

Riliwa sighed. Quietly, with her eyes down, she replied, 'Nobody is saying you can't talk, Mama, but why must there be an argument about London every day? You think if I was not looking for money and work to better our lives, I would be leaving my child behind? You think if I had a husband, I would be doing this? Do you think this is easy for me? Do I know when I will next see my son? Will he even know me again?' She swallowed the knot in her throat as she tied a white plastic bag that held some of her slippers and placed them in the suitcase. She briefly looked up at her mother who was now silent, her features softened. 'Mama, I thought you said you wanted to help me pack?' Her mother joined her in rearranging the contents of her luggage so they wouldn't need to sit on the case just to close it.

Mary's place was on the other side of London. It was not a particularly fancy area and her three-bedroom council flat was on the fourteenth floor of a brutalist structure that formed part of a mammoth, notorious estate. Riliwa dreaded her encounters with nebulous characters in the old lift that was as cramped as a coffin and always smelt like a combination of menstrual blood and Benson & Hedges cigarettes. Inside Mary's flat, however, was a world away. Riliwa had not been there for a few months, and she noticed the place had been redecorated. The deep, fluffy, peach carpets matched both the chintzy striped, floral wallpaper and the plump leather three-piece suite the shade of a pale cantaloupe. However, it was the expensive Sony television – on a black and gold multilayered stand – to match the side and centre table – that immediately drew the eye. This, and the ostentatious eight-arm faux-crystal chandelier hanging from the ceiling that was so impossibly overbearing it couldn't help but announce its presence.

'You've changed the place!' Riliwa said.

'Ah, thank you, o, my sister. It's nice, eh?' Mary replied, smiling proudly...

'Yes, very beautiful.' replied Riliwa with awe in her voice. Because, unless she wanted to be accused of jealousy, she knew that was what was expected of her. What was not expected of Riliwa, was to ask exactly where all the money had come from because she never saw Mary going to work. But Riliwa knew. Mary had a nose for business; she was excellent at fraud. Whether it was knowing the tricks to snagging a council house from the government or very realistic fake documents, Mary had the answers. And if she didn't, she always knew someone who did. And she would always, *always* take her cut. Riliwa took off her shoes in the hallway. This ritual, where any guests had to take off their shoes before entering any of the rooms, was one of the only clues to Mary's Muslim background.

They'd first met at school. Even though they were never close, Riliwa knew then that Mary had plans for her life that were far bigger than anything Osun State had to offer. Back then, she was called Mariama. Anglicizing her name, she later explained to Riliwa on one of her visits home from London, was necessary for success in the UK. It was why in the documents she procured for her that Riliwa's name was now Rachel. 'At least you still have your name starting with the same letter, so you won't forget it'. But Riliwa did forget it, once staring ahead blankly as a voice calling 'Rachel, Rachel!'

sounded out behind her. When her work colleague caught up with her and asked why she didn't reply when called, Riliwa clumsily apologized, claiming to have had something on her mind. Which was partly true. But she was so aware how terrible the repercussions could have been if her colleague realized she wasn't who she said she was. She had heard stories of people being deported from their workplaces with just the clothes on their back.

Riliwa looked at Mary beaming with pride at her redecorated apartment. She was almost thirty, had a six-year-old child with her problematic ex-lover, was rarely without gum in her mouth and wore, without fail, tight, skimpy clothing. Today, despite it being cold outside, she wore a denim bra top with gold buckles and a kaleidoscopic pair of spandex leggings that were not high-waisted enough to hide the creases of the grey and silver stretch marks across her slightly puffy brown stomach. Riliwa always felt she was trying to look a little like those yardie girls but regardless of how coloured her extensions were and the number of rhinestones she encrusted onto her fake nails, she still looked Nigerian. Her broad nose and the tiny but distinct tribal marks on each of her cheeks were a giveaway.

Mary led the way to the (new) kitchen diner in her spacious flat. 'So, how now, Riliwa? Where have you been since? How is the new place?' Mary opened the fridge. 'Coke, Sprite or Fanta?'

'Sprite, thank you,' replied Riliwa. 'I'm fine. The new place is fine. I mean it's not the best but I couldn't stay at your place forever.'

'Ah ah,' said Mary, her face feigning hurt. 'I wasn't chasing you from here. You know you could have stayed here for as long as you needed.'

'Yes, I know, thank you, and I'm grateful... At least I am now closer to work,' Riliwa said as she took a swig from her can. One day, six months into her being in London, she came back from her evening cleaning job to find a police car outside the house. She kept on walking, her heart beating so rapidly she thought it would physically stop. She walked as far as her legs would carry her in the brute cold. It was only when she realized she had been walking for around two hours that she finally decided to make her way back. When she saw that the police car was nowhere to be seen, she ventured down her road and into the house. It turns out the neighbours had called the police in response to the violent screams coming from the room across from hers, which was occupied by a Spanish couple. She too had heard their fights and saw the bruises on Dolores's face and chest. But then Riliwa would also see how loved-up Dolores and Alejandro were and so she decided to pretend she was blind and deaf. The Belgian Congolese student who had the room next to the couple told Riliwa that the police had taken Alejandro away that night, and this time, Dolores's injuries were so bad she had been admitted into hospital. They were all shaken by the incident, so much so that Riliwa was afraid to keep staying there. What if the police came back? Mary offered her the spare bedroom until she could find somewhere else to live.

But of course, nothing Mary did was for free. In addition to paying for lodging and paying off the fee for the fake work documents, Riliwa was also Mary's unpaid childcare and cleaning service. But it was the unwanted sexual advances of Mary's on-off boyfriend, despite her purposely wearing unattractive, non-descript, shapeless clothing, that finally forced her out. Of course, this is not something she shared with her friend. She was only here because she understood they were no longer together. And she needed to use a land-line that wasn't in a cold, filthy phonebooth.

Riliwa looked at the time. 'Ah, Mama will be waiting. Please can I ring her now?' She handed Mary thirty pounds as payment for the service and Mary handed her the cordless phone.

'Mama, how are you?' she began, once she heard her mother say hello. The line wasn't perfect but she could hear her mother relief in hearing her daughter's voice. She excitedly updated Riliwa on everything happening in the neighbourhood, who was having a baby, who had left to go to Lagos, whose husband was cheating, whose child got accepted into a good school, which random person died.

Riliwa was happy to indulge in banal gossip; it took her away from the bleakness of her current life. Her mother also put Riliwa's young son on the phone. Hearing his voice broke and blessed Riliwa in equal measure but she held it all in until she hung up ten minutes later. Mary sat down and put her hands around Riliwa's shoulders as she sobbed.

'I know, I know, these years have been hard. Only God can help us in this country. But...' Mary took a breath. 'I know you said you don't want to do it but if you can get your full papers, you will be able to visit home without problems, you will be able to get a better job, a better place to live; more money. And you'll be able to send for Jimoh; he can start school here.'

Riliwa wiped her eyes. 'Where will I find five-thousand pounds to pay for someone to marry me so I can get my stay? You make it sound as if it is so easy.'

'Okay,' Mary said decisively. 'I will lend you the money. You can pay it back in time.'

'No, no, no.' Riliwa shook her head. 'How will I pay you back? The one I owe you, I am still paying. No, I can't. I don't want to keep owing you like that. I can't.'

'So, you don't want to visit home?' Mary retorted. 'You don't want to see Jimoh until when? Till he is eighteen? Are you going to just stay in the UK as an illegal? So that every time you see police you soil your underwear? What kind of life is that?' Mary now sounded bewildered and irritated. It wasn't the first time they'd had the conversation. Riliwa had always wanted to find a way to do things properly. But years of worrying around her legal status had left her exhausted. It didn't matter that she'd practised her annunciation to loosen her thick accent, that she had mastered remembering that her name was now Rachel Williams and not Riliwa Momodu, that she knew Rachel's national insurance number by heart and had the documentation to prove it, that she had a home – albeit atrocious – where the landlord didn't pry and only cared about the rent being paid on time. It wasn't enough. She didn't feel safe. Since her student visa had run out, her effort to disappear while remaining in the UK, all while constantly looking over her shoulder, was beginning to take its toll. She had of course heard of the many Africans and Jamaicans in sham marriages. The interview process at the hands of the Home Office sounded terrifying. And many didn't end well. But what were her options to move her life beyond where she was now? She was in no position to bring her son to join her. And she couldn't go back home. She was beginning to get desperate.

'But how will I find the money?' asked Riliwa. Her menial cleaning jobs – one at a bingo hall, the other, an office – in the morning and evening was barely enough to scrape by. 'By the time I pay the rent, bills, buy food, send money home for Jimoh...' She began sobbing again.

'*Oya, oya*, Riliwa, I beg, let's stop all these tears. This is not the time for crying.' Mary was becoming increasingly impatient. 'The first thing we need to do is get some documents together so we can apply for benefits for you. The money from that will help to pay back the loan and of course the fees for arranging these documents for the marriage. What do you have to lose? It's not like you even have to work for the money. Do you know how many single people that are collecting A LOT of money from the government? Not just for themselves but also for their four children that they don't even have. All this working like a dog every day, it's not necessary. There are different ways to live in this country.'

Riliwa looked at her friend, slightly bewildered.

Mary rolled her eyes. 'Riliwa, you better stop all this innocent nonsense. Do you want to live in one dirty room for the rest of your life? You have to do what is necessary to do more than just survive. You think all this –' she said, her hand motioning across the room '– just *happened* because I was sitting on a chair crying? I had to find a way. I know how hard it is for our people when they come here. I know how hard it was for me. England is *hard*. But I now understand the system. That's why I helped you, that's why I help others.' She chuckled, 'Why do you think they call me Hail Mary?'

As Mary put her case forward for sainthood, Riliwa bit her lip. She wasn't aware of the minutiae of Mary's criminal activities, but she had long observed how altruistic Mary was.

Which is why she was nervous about borrowing that money from her. Whatever deals there were to be made, Mary would most certainly be getting a cut from it. And Riliwa would still be expected to pay interest. High interest. At this rate, she would be indebted to Mary forever. But what choice did she have?

'So,' she said finally, resigned. 'What do I need to do?'

'Eh heh! Now you are seeing sense! Okay.' Mary stood up. 'Stay there, let me make a call.' She went off into her bedroom and closed the door. Riliwa sunk her feet deeper into the plush carpet and locked eyes with the blackness of the mammoth TV screen. She stared back at her reflection and thought of how much these surroundings contrasted with her own tiny room with its thin, frayed burgundy carpet and the damp on the walls that no amount of bleach would or could get rid of.

Mary reappeared ten minutes later. 'If you can come back here next Sunday around this same time, with some passport photographs and the NI card I gave you, we can start the process. My friend will be here to collect everything.' Riliwa nodded. Before she could respond, she heard a key in the lock of the main door and the sound of a man's and a child's voice. It was Mary's ex. They were obviously back together.

'Aunty Rachel!' The little boy's eyes lit up when he spotted Riliwa. He was about to run into the living room when his mother blocked the doorway 'David, how many times do I need to tell you to take your shoes off?' He kicked off his shoes and ran over to Riliwa, almost knocking her over with the force of his hug. He had always been such a sweet, spirited boy. She initially didn't understand why a Muslim woman from Ondo State would give her child a non-African name and a Christian one, at that. After being in London for a few years, she understood. She understood the necessity of not standing out with a name that no one could pronounce. A name people would baulk at and then mock. So, you do whatever you need to do to assimilate. It was the only way to survive.

'Aunty, where have you been? I have a new PlayStation!' She smiled at him and stroked his face. Seeing him always made her yearn for her own son but after her conversation with Mary and the possibilities it presented, her yearning felt less painful.

'Look at you, you're a big boy now. How is school?'

David made a face. 'School is boring.' He grabbed her hand and began trying to pull her out of her seat. 'Come and see the new PlayStation.' Mary's boyfriend walked in and reached over to squeeze his girlfriend's rear. Riliwa looked away. He grabbed the remote control and sat dramatically in the chair opposite Riliwa.

'Long time,' he said evenly, staring at her.

'Yes, long time. Good evening,' she replied formally, standing up.

Aunty Rachel has to go home, David,' said Mary. The atmosphere was now taut and neither the sound of an innocent child nor the racket from Mary's baby father's channel-hopping was going to change that. 'It's getting late, and she has far to go,' explained his mother, in response to David's disappointed face. 'But she'll be here next week, won't you?'

Riliwa nodded cheerfully, hugging the boy as she walked towards the hallway. She put her shoes on and grabbed her coat. 'Yes, I'll be here next week. You can show me your PlayStation then. Okay?'

In the days that followed, everything for Riliwa felt so much more bearable, a stark contrast to the preceding week which had felt particularly tough. Mother's Day always did. It amazed her how much England was lauded and celebrated back home. Her reality was cruel and cold. But as she looked forward to everything Mary had proposed, it felt less so. Even Riliwa's weekly ritual of wiping mould from the side of her bed, cooking in the chaos of the shared kitchen which had recently had a maggot outbreak, leaving the house at 4:00A.M. so she could take two night buses to get to her cleaning job, it all felt less arduous because of the hope she now had. She could finally see a way forward, a way out, a way to bring Jimoh to be with her.

On Saturday night, Riliwa found herself humming 'Seun Rere'. Whenever her son was restless, tired, upset, she would rock him in her arms, singing the Christy Essien Igbokwe song. It never failed to settle him. Usually, she would recall those moments and find herself spiralling into sadness. But not tonight. Her son would be back in her arms soon.

Transport on a Sunday was notoriously slow, and since Riliwa had a long way to go, she planned an early start. Her bag – with everything Mary had asked her to bring – was already packed. Before leaving, she went into the kitchen to make a cup of tea to warm her up before heading out into the cold. The excitement – and nerves – had taken away her appetite. She gulped down her tea standing up and as she headed towards the door, bumped into Mustafa. '*Salaam Alaikum*,' she greeted him with a smile. He seemed surprised but nevertheless greeted her back. She went to catch the first bus – she needed three to get to Mary's. The train was much quicker but also more expensive and she needed to save every penny.

Riliwa walked into Mary's building and called for the lift. The smell was as offensive as usual. She pressed the fourteenth floor. The doors opened on what looked like the wrong floor. She pressed 14 again. The lift stayed where it was. Riliwa stepped out, confused. She could see the 'Welcome' doormat and she could see what looked like Mary's door. At least, where Mary's door usually was. But it didn't *look* like Mary's door. It had been barricaded with what looked like a thick steel overlay with brown nails hammered in all around the sides. Riliwa walked tentatively towards it and knocked. Subtly at first and then harder. 'Mary? Mary! It's me! Are you there? Mary?' A door on the other side of the small landing creaked opened. It was the old Jamaican neighbour.

'Darling, you is wasting you time,' she said wearily. 'Nobody is there. I don't know what was going on, but Tuesday night immigration come and them kicked down the door. Police, everyting. Lawd Gad, it was a *whole* loop a drama,' she said her eyes wide, shaking her head.

'So...so...so...' 'Riliwa was struggling to find her words. 'So, where is Mary? Where is she? she finally managed. The woman raised her eyebrow. 'Me no know but the people them take she, her man, the pickney, some other people... I don't know where them gone. But this is why I tell the young people dem, you can't come to England and think you can fleece the system, it a go catch up pon you. Me tell them...' Rilliwa could no longer hear what she was saying. She began to walk back to the lift, but her legs felt like lead. Her hand shook as she pressed G. She could no longer smell the odour.

When she got out of the building Riliwa headed to the local store to top up her phone credit. She dialled Mary's number. *You have dialled an incorrect number* came the response. She tried again and again and again: *You have dialled an incorrect number. You have dialled an incorrect number.* She crumbled into a heap on the side of the pavement and just sat there oblivious to the passersby who gave her strange looks. She simply stared, too stunned to cry. Finally, she got up and headed back home. As she put her key in the door, she saw Mustafa with his boyfriend. 'Salaam Alaikum,' he greeted her with a wide smile. She looked past him, went to her room and shut the door firmly behind her.

DODO IS YORUBA
FOR FRIED PLANTAIN

Six weeks ago, Morayo buried her husband in Gloucestershire. The plot of land had been in his family for generations. A plot of land reserved for occasions such as this. And so there he lay, with his mother and maternal grandparents. His philandering father, long separated from his mother and detached from his children, was buried in the London Brompton cemetery. It was the one closest to his Chelsea flat, a beautiful bachelor pad where he finally died in his sleep after years of suffering from dementia. It was a condition that was originally self-imposed (he preferred to believe his family didn't exist) and, in his latter years, medically diagnosed.

After her husband's funeral, Morayo's house, once hers and her husband's, now just hers, had been a cacophony of clattering crockery, nostalgic storytelling, and laughter. It felt apt; Morayo's husband had a dry, sharp sense of humor. It was one of the reasons she fell for him. He was smart, charming, not as tall as she'd like – in her high heels, they were the same height – but goodness, a dream to look at. When they first became friends – two outcasts from completely different worlds bonding in the university library over a love of Oscar Wilde – she was alarmed at how clear he was in his desire to date her. He wasn't intimidated by her strong features, her short hair, her coal-like hue… It was strange but exciting, flattering but also overwhelming. And so she said many 'no's before she finally said yes; his wit became too difficult to resist. Only years down the line did she realize the mirth was a blanket for his pain.

The laughter that emanated from the mourners at the repast was much more transparent, almost gossamer-thin. It petered into a deep sigh, the watering of the eyes, quivering snuffles. All eventually punctuated with a silence that no words could fill. Those silences and sounds – and the people that made them – were now long gone at Morayo's insistence. She lied when she told everyone she just wanted life to get 'back to normal'. She wasn't sure the 'normal' she had with her husband was normal. Be it his normal. Or even hers. Whatever it was, she knew she no longer wanted it. She also knew she didn't want to spend the building blocks of this new stage of her life wrapped up in someone else's. Hence, she refused her eldest daughter's pleas to cross the Atlantic and move in with her young family. Charlotte (Morayo now wonders why she didn't insist on Yoruba names for her children. No real Nigerian is called Charlotte) lived in a huge apartment on the Upper East Side in New York where she worked in publishing. Her husband made his money in banking. Elodie and Maria – their fair, racially ambiguous twin children – betrayed none of their African roots.

Her own husband's body was barely cold before Morayo's brother and sister began preparing the spare rooms in their respective London homes. After the service, the siblings continued to battle protectively over her, as if she were invisible. She shouted her dissent at them, immediately inviting the earlier silence back into the room. They forgave her at once despite the fact she did not ask for their forgiveness.

Morayo also turned down her husband's sister's polite but insincere request for her to come to stay, 'at least till things start to make sense.' Morayo's laugh was wry. Things stopped making sense a long time ago. But she said nothing as she shook her head. She had never cared much for the company of her high- maintenance sister-in-law, who, desperate to fill the gap long left by their father, had always competed with Morayo for her brother's attention.

She sat in her marital bedroom – her husband's signature cologne (*Floris* No. 89) still permeated the air – listening to Bella suggest that she leave the large Chelsea flat given to her by her father – which she now shared with her fiancé – to keep her mother company – 'even if it is just for a few months...' Morayo chuckled, raising her brows as she wiped her younger daughter's damp cheeks. 'Ha! You've changed your tune! Who would have thought it? You couldn't wait to leave home, remember? 'Oh, I hate this place.! As soon as I'm eighteen, I'm out!' Bella laughed softly at her mother's gentle jesting recalling her rebellious years.

'Darling,' Morayo's voice lowered as she looked her daughter in the eye, 'it's pointless moving back home.'

'Yes, I know, but—'

Morayo raised her hand, interjecting to counter Bella's protest. 'I know it's just for a few months, but you've always dreamed of your independence, and –' she waved the back of her hand in the air '– you don't want to be stuck here with me. I promise I won't be lonely. Besides, there's so much to sort out to keep me busy. Honestly, I'll be fine'. She smiled sadly as she stroked her daughter's not quite afro but not quite Caucasian hair. It's the kind of Black hair, observed Morayo, that both Black and white people were comfortable with. It was palatably Black. 'Also,' she added, with faux cheer, 'Have you forgotten, there's also that small issue of a wedding to plan?'

Bella now wept freely. 'He's gone Mum. He won't be there. He's gone.'

The finality of those words began to splinter Morayo, but she defied the pull to crumble. So instead, she scoffed. 'I bet you right now he's saying, 'Ah, my plan worked, you're *my* daughter, why on earth would I want to give you away to someone else?!''

Despite herself, Bella laughed, 'Yes, you're right, knowing him...' She drifted off.

Knowing him, thought Morayo. Did she truly ever really know him? Perhaps if she did, they never would have got married. After a long pause, she found herself quoting a scripture her mother used often: '*But this one thing I do, forgetting those things which are behind, and reaching forth unto those things which are before...*' Her daughter looked at her, slightly quizzical. 'We have to look forward,' Morayo said decisively. 'Do we have a choice?'

Her daughter looked down without responding but she understood this was not a question. Rather, it was a statement. And that was that.

So today, here she was. In Brixton. Heading towards the market. A day after the house had finally emptied of the stream of visitors, she started to develop a craving for *dodo*. In her head she still called plantain by its Yoruba name. While she had now spent most of her life living in Britain, the anglicizing of something so rooted and grounded in her

Lagos childhood felt odd. 'Dodo is Yoruba for fried plantain,' she remembered explaining to her husband. Now, she
found herself also hungrily considering *jollof* rice, fried giz-
zard, *amala* with okra soup, *moi moi*, steamed goat meat,
perfected in its own juices with just a little salt and finely
sliced rings of onions. As children, she and her brother
were always stealing goat meat from the pot, especially
during the time their mother was too consumed with nurs-
ing their baby sister to pay much attention to anything else
happening in the house. Morayo became an expert at lifting
and placing the lid back down without it making a single
sound. Like a ballet-dancing criminal, she would furtively
sway back to her bedroom on tiptoes, meat in hand, before
their mother came out of the sitting room. Morayo always
got away with it. Her brother was not so skilled. Once, he
had just put a small piece of goat in his mouth when their
mother unexpectedly walked into the kitchen. She was
initially oblivious to the misdemeanour, but he'd looked so
suspicious she asked him what he was hiding. In his panic,
he tried to swallow the meat whole and ended up nearly
passing out when it lodged in his throat.

Morayo's appetite grew and she began to hanker after
ikokore. As with the *dodo* principle, in her head it was always
'*ikokore*', never water yam porridge. She found this craving
alarming considering she had always detested it. Perhaps
her early hatred stemmed from the smell of the smoked fish

her grandmother generously added to the dish. Or maybe it was because all her primary school classmates spread the vicious rumour that Iya Bisi, the woman famed for cooking *Ikokore* in their hometown, Ikenne, was a witch that devoured strange charms to bind the womb of her husband's young mistress. This mistress was a flamboyant, bold-as-brass woman who made no attempt to hide the fact she was 'the other woman'. Morayo and her fellow eight-year-olds were increasingly horrified as they observed the mistress's humongous swell – by now solid as concrete – continuing in its expansion with no real-life baby on the horizon. 'It's been three years already! And no baby has come out!!' they whispered amongst themselves, horrified. Hence it was said that if you ate *Ikokore*, the same would become of you. Morayo's smile was slight as she remembered their naivety. At their age, nine months did seem like three years.

She came to the first store. Morayo stroked the fresh plantain longingly, picking one up and inspecting it as one looking for clues at a crime scene. She had watched her mother doing the same, although back then she was never quite sure what her mother was looking for. This was all too evident the first time Morayo came home with the bag of plantain she was sent to buy. Her mother's face fell. 'Ah! Does this look good to you? Look at all these black black marks… where did you get this from? Thin here, big in the middle…like someone suffering from kwashiorkor.

And this one here, eh!! It's not ripe yet! Did they blindfold you at the market? Can't you see?! It's dodo we are trying to make, not plantain crisps. Or you want your father to break his teeth?!'

'Special offer for you today darling! Six for one pound.' The Asian man of indistinguishable age held his arms open towards all the women scrutinizing the fresh vegetables and herbs at the front of his store. A light-skinned speckled-faced Jamaican woman (Morayo noted her accent; in her ears it was clearly distinct from her fellow Caribbeans) caught his attention so she could place her order first. Morayo's eyes took in the market. From her vantage point, she could see at least four other shops displaying heaps of plantain on the stalls outside their shops. It was plantain season. She could hear her mother's voice – 'Make sure you don't buy from the first place. You must look around and see who has the best ones. The people from the first shop are thieves.' Morayo was sure the shop would have changed ownership since her mother spoke those words to her all those years ago. Besides, she lacked the patience to walk around searching for 'perfect plantains' in a sea of plantains that, to her eyes, looked pretty identical. The Asian man now placed his attention on Morayo. 'We also have very plenty fresh thyme, okra, hot *pepa* for your stew...' He paused and looked her up and down, taking in what she was wearing. Her ensemble, a smart green-velvet dress with shiny courts admittedly did feel out of place on a Tuesday morning in Brixton market. He squinted inquisitively as if trying to place her. 'You are Nigeria?' His grammatical error triggered her memory. Morayo's husband, always so particular about the use of the English language, would have found it both hilarious and infuriating at the same time. He would have teased her about it endlessly. 'Joy (for, ever since she told him it was the English translation of her name, that's what he called her), you are Nigeria? Yes, Joy, of course you are Nigeria! You are a country not a human being! You are Nigeria!' And perhaps they would roll around in bed, him showering her with ostentatious kisses, both of them giggling like teenagers, her secretly quelling the discomfort she felt about this white man's, perhaps inadvertent, derision of her fellow immigrant.

'Yes,' she replied to the man. It was pointless – and rude – correcting him.

'Ah ha!' The sudden spark in his eyes and close-lipped smile, both self-congratulatory signifiers. He delved further. 'So, you are…Yoruba?'

This time it was she who smiled. 'Yes.'

To which he said proudly, 'Ah, I know. I am here, very long time, and I see many people… You…you different. But I know.'

Morayo was silently impressed. In the Cotswolds village where she had lived for close to twenty-five years, distinctions were not made between Africans, West Indians, Black

Americans, much less them taking an interest as to which country and tribe she was from. She was just Black. Or for those of a certain ilk, she was 'coloured'. Which in their mind meant many, many things. Very early on, she found herself melding so far into the security of her husband, hoping to cast the care of her melanin count. But there were too many cutting reminders. She found it exhausting relaying this to her husband. An innocent question from an old childhood friend she'd caught up with after many years kept coming back to her: 'How do you cope with sharing the rest of your life with someone who could never know what it's like to exist in this world as a Black person?' How she coped was by giving up trying to explain everything to her husband and instead she began keeping the layers of racist lacerations she acquired over the years hidden under ever more layers. Morayo had no idea she wasn't the only one mastering the art of suppressing what truly lay beneath.

'*Ekaabo*! Okay, what you want to buy today?' The Indian man pointed to the hot round small peppers. 'We have *ata rodo*.' Relishing the sound of his Yoruba, Morayo couldn't help but beam. She commended his welcome in her native tongue. If he really was from a line of crooks, as her mother said, he was a very charming one.

'Right, perhaps we start there,' she replied to the man, pointing to the pyramid of yams too high for her to reach. 'No, not that one. No, move your hand that way – yes to the right, a bit more, the one next to it. Yes, that one. Half will do fine. Thank you.'

He chopped the yam, bagged it and beckoned for her to hand over the plantain that had initially caught her attention. She quickly picked up six of them – the ones that had the least black marks and bruises, hopefully her mother would approve – and handed them to him. She grabbed two sprigs of thyme and small brown paper bags which she filled with okra, fresh tomatoes and the *ata rodos* the man had directed her to. Walking further into the shop, her heart leapt with excitement as she spotted a row of palm oil in small kegs. She hadn't set eyes on that in a long while. The man watched curiously as she approached them like the prodigal son's father and added it to her pile of foods which now included ewedu leaf, black eyed beans, egusi seeds, a small bag of *amala*; the shade of grey disguising the marvellous purple it would turn once steeped in hot water… The man began packing them all into bags as he tallied up her bill.

'Finish?' he queried. Morayo's eyes flitted around the stall/shop, undecided.

'What about some *garri*?' He pointed to the bags of cassava. 'New delivery. Just for you. I do you a good price.' He grinned widely as he brazenly attempted to lure her with his wares. His overlapping brown tooth, earlier obscured by his thick moustache, was now on full show. Morayo remembered her mother's warning and smiled. She put her palm out and said, 'No, thank you, I'm okay. I have enough.' The man pretended to be offended. 'Ah, you no like my shop? Why it's enough, Yoruba woman, why?'

She laughed, playing along with him 'It's enough, it's enough.'

'*O ti to?*' he asked, showcasing his Yoruba once again.

'Yes,' she agreed as she paid him, increasingly impressed by his Yoruba. '*O ti to.* It's enough.'

A young boy – she assumed it was the man's son – helped place the bags into her trolley. It was almost full. Thank goodness it has wheels, she thought. She had not carried heavy bags for years. Her husband was quite the gentleman and wouldn't allow it. Not that she could ever imagine him in Brixton market. There were many places of course she could never imagine him inhabiting. And yet…

Morayo thanked the boy and waved the man goodbye. '*Odabo,*' he replied cheerily.

She smiled as she walked away. '*Odabo,*' she replied in a voice she herself barely recognized. It felt strange speaking Yoruba. There he was, an Indian man with no African blood in him, happily telling her goodbye in *her* own tongue, savouring the words as he spoke them and yet she herself had not spoken those words in years and so of course her own children – flesh of her flesh, bone of her bone – had never uttered a single word in Yoruba. And never revealed any desire to do so. Where on earth were you when this was

happening?' her inside voice scolded her. Morayo felt queasy
with shame.

She slowly walked past the numerous halal butchers,
their bloodied meats filling the market. Some of the butchers called out to her, 'Come, darling, we have meat for your
pepper soup. Nice meat.' She hadn't eaten pepper soup in
years. Her mother would make it when they lived in Ikoyi in
Lagos. But she actually preferred to eat it at Amaka's house.
Her Igbo friend's mother made the best pepper soup.

'You want some goat meat, madam? Goat meat? Very
nice. Just for you. Fresh, fresh.' She was tempted. It did look
fresh. She still needed to buy meat to go in her stew. Because,
as a bewildered aunt once said to her, 'Who eats *amala* with
stew and okra and *no meat*?' Yet she couldn't bear to buy it
from them. Even now, meat that, according to her mother
'had been sacrificed to an alien god', was suspicious to her.
After she, her siblings and parents came back to settle in
London, they would still travel to Nigeria on occasion. It
was then, on these rare and infrequent visits, that Morayo's
Catholic-raised mother began to educate her children on
how 'people use food as a tool for spiritual battles'. Her
mother threw away countless bowls of food that had been
brought over by her unbelieving in-laws 'as a token of our
love', or 'as a gift', or 'just to greet you' or 'to welcome you
home'. Her mother would smile a smile as insincere as the
heart of the givers, thanking them for their thoughtfulness.

Once they left, she would laugh victoriously 'Witches! Who do they think they can fool? Who is going to eat this food that has been marinating in the *babalawo's* house since the day I married your father? God punish them! These illiterates will not kill me.' And down the toilet, it went. Flushed down with acid.

Morayo dragged her trolley behind her and suddenly remembered the West Indian butcher's at the corner of Atlantic Road. She hoped it was still there. It was. Run by the dour-faced Jamaicans who barely looked at their customers as they took payment and irritably chastened the indecisive and the ignorant who couldn't choose between stewing mutton and curry goat. This time it was Morayo's father's voice that came back to her. 'Ah, those West Indians...' When he first came to England, the contention between West Indians and Africans was rife. She heard stories of Nigerians who dated Caribbeans that were ostracized by their shocked families. Ironically, despite (or perhaps due to) seeing and experiencing the effects of colonial rule, they were more forgiving at the idea of those who were dating a white person. Which is why, when she began sleeping with an older Jamaican boy at sixteen, she kept her lover a secret. Their clandestine trysts still sent shivers up her spine. As time went by, a gulf began to emerge between them: she sought out university in Edinburgh, curious to see what a world beyond hers would bring. He, on the other hand, had get-rich-quick plans that, in her mind, looked unlikely to take him beyond south east London. Ultimately however, it was the deep-rooted superiority complex his family had towards Africans that Morayo lost patience for. Even at their first meeting, his mother made it clear she found Morayo's hair texture objectionable. 'We have always had *pretty* hair in this family. *Always.* My grandfather was half Indian, you know,' she announced proudly. Hers was a barely hidden vitriol that far superseded any prejudice her own father had exhibited. She and her Jamaican lover officially parted the summer after she began university. Two years later, she met her husband.

Morayo stuffed the plastic bag of meats inside her trolley, zipped it up and walked towards the back of the market where she had parked. She was always commended on how well she drove. It helped that at her age she still had 20/20 vision. She intended to keep it that way. After the painful experience of slowly watching her father going blind, she became obsessive about looking after her eyes.

That week, Morayo spent much of her time doing something she had not done for a long time: cook. And then she feasted. Black-eyed beans with corn and *dodo*, jollof rice with *moi moi* and fried spicy chicken. She was delighted that she could now buy ready-packaged bean powder which only required her to add water. Her mother, ever the purist, would have baulked at the idea of creating *moi moi* from the

73

ambiguous contents of a plastic packet. Morayo knew, of course, that if she ground the beans from scratch, the *moi moi* would have tasted even better. She also knew it would take forever. Bean powder *moi moi* suited her just fine. On Sunday, she cooked the yam – sliced into great chunky circles – in salt and sugar water, just like Sikirat, their cook, would make for the family when they were in Lagos. It went beautifully with the eggs she beat and fried with sardines, plum tomatoes, thyme, salt, onions and peppers. The more Morayo ate, the more her appetite expanded. She even woke up in anticipation of what was to pass her lips that day. Breakfast was the remaining yam eaten with a simple but generous drizzle of palm oil. Later on in the day, she enjoyed another one of her childhood favorites; just cupping soft mounds of amala *and* dipping the purplish grey cassava into a stew of okra and assorted meats invigorated her. She wished she had an old 45 of Ebenezer Obey playing in the background. She thought of the 'big men' in Nigeria eating various *okele* and stew at parties while Obey or Ayinla Kollington played – always far too loudly, of course – with their live band. Morayo's husband never saw her eat *amala* or any kind of *okele*. He was too concerned with etiquette. They never ate Nigerian food together after they were married. But she pined for it. And she pined for Nigeria. She would pine, despite the mosquitoes, which at best would bite and blight your skin with thick itchy lumps and at worst gave you malaria. She would pine, disregarding the fact that NEPA was always 'taking the light', thereby leaving you to find your way around the house with dull mustard-flamed lanterns and candles. She would pine, even though the threat of armed robbers and area boys was omnipresent. The pining wasn't constant of course – assimilation was essential for survival in Britain – so she became skilled in suppressing the ebbs and flows. The first argument she had with her husband centred around jollof rice. Polishing off a plate of it at a Nigerian party she had summoned the courage to take him to, he said how delicious it was and joked about the high level of fat contained in the African foods. No wonder he laughed as he watched amused, without desire, the women dancing in their lace outfits, with 'bottoms you could land planes on'.

Once they were married, Morayo's husband monopolized the kitchen. This, a rarity in her upbringing, in her culture, was considered a blessing – especially when the children came. Both friends and family envied her, including her mother. 'Which African man do you think you would marry that will cook *and* serve his wife food? Morayo, you truly have seen joy. Your life is living up to your name.'

Her husband cooked delicious meals – usually centred around meat from the best butchers. His parents had owned a huge farm in Gloucestershire; he knew 'good meat'. He knew 'good food' and spent all his spare time making it. On one occasion, she insisted they stop by Fonthill Road market while they were on their way back from visiting an old crony of his that had recently returned to live in central London after many years in the Far East. She wanted to buy some plantain. Her husband didn't, complaining that they'd get stuck in traffic (which they did). Perhaps it was an afternoon spent in the presence of a couple who still pronounced Kenya 'Keen-ya', *but* there was an indignation rising in Morayo. So, despite her husbands' protesting, she was fierce in her insistence. She bought and later fried and ate her plantain alone. The enjoyment of the food was spoilt by the atmosphere of disapproval her husband created. He sat quietly in the room, with a dour face... That was the last time she cooked Nigerian food in the house. And now, as she smacked her lips, licking the okra stew from her fingers, her eyes watered and burned. She mourned that her children had never developed a palette for Nigerian food, and yet they were half Nigerian. They had Nigerian blood and yet had never set foot on the land. They had no Nigerian middle names and even if they did, they were highly unlikely to pronounce them correctly, their enunciation would be all wrong. As a young girl about to leave Nigeria for London, uncles and aunties were generous in throwing unrequested pieces of advice at her. One in particular said, 'Don't marry one of those *oyibos,* oh! How will your children know who we are? If you marry one of them, we won't see you again. So, when the time comes, return home and marry one of our own. East or West, home is the best.' As a married woman she only visited Nigeria twice. On both occasions, it was when her parents, who, aside from the odd trips back to London, had long fulfilled their desire to resettle back home, passed away. After that, Morayo's husband had little interest in regularly travelling thousands of miles to visit aunties, uncles, cousins and ex house helps from her youth – people he didn't know.

Over the years, the images and stories portrayed in the media had not helped her case. Her husband would counter: *It's too dangerous. I don't think we should be compromising the children's safety. Also, there's poverty...and then us flaunting our Western privileges that we so take for granted...it's not right...it would be obscene. And of course, there's malaria...* Morayo consoled herself with the knowledge that this was the sacrifice women who married outside their tribes made. She was not the first. Her own mother tongue and land were foreign to her. When people asked which tribe she was from, she automatically answered, 'Yoruba' – her father's ethnic group. She never said, 'Oh, and I'm half Itsekiri.' Her mother's culture became inconsequential. It was simply the way it was. Just as Morayo's mother seemed to accept it – if it was a problem, she certainly didn't mention it – Morayo found herself following her mother's example, accepting her own path. Her mother – and others – would have considered Morayo's discontent ungrateful. Was it really that bad? And if so, surely she had eyes, what had she been looking at? She had a mouth, could she not have spoken? To everyone else, Morayo lived a good – no, a great – life in the grand country home they moved to after years in London. What could she have wanted for? Her husband was a great provider, a loving, kind man, the father of her beautiful children, her best friend…

And now he was dead. What no one knew was, the man they knew to be her husband died a long time ago. Perhaps he never even existed. She often looked back and questioned why she ignored the red flags. Perhaps the truth was just too terrifying to digest. There was something, so many *some-things* she couldn't quite place. It was like permanently trying to adjust one's eyes in the dark…and trying, and trying… Who *really* were those men – younger, older, sometimes foreign – that he introduced to her as 'old friends'? What were those odd looks exchanged between them, between him and others at their dinner parties, like a private code that could only be deciphered by the eyes of the beholders? There were the odd nights where he would disappear for hours, only to re-emerge on a high and then a low that was drenched in contempt. And there were the excuses. He didn't want to be touched. 'I'm sorry, I'm just tired… Yes, I know it's been a while…' And just when she thought she knew, there were moments that caused confusion. When he told her how much he loved her, his voice hoarse, his eyes burning with honesty. When he reacted possessively or jealously when he thought men were flirting with her. 'He can go and get his own fucking wife,' he raged after one particularly awkward dinner party where she reluctantly agreed to 'just one' dance with a family friend. When he made love to her, so intensely, so passionately, calling her name as if his life depended on it. But when she convinced herself, all was well, there was that *something* again. As she confronted him, questioning him for the final time about 'Mark,' a mysterious man who kept calling the house, who her husband had simply dismissed as a colleague at his law firm. As she, showing him, hands shaking, the half ripped empty condom packet she found in his pocket – they never used condoms – both their worlds fell apart. He begged her for grace, for forgiveness, for help. They both wept, both filled with a desperate, wretched self-loathing and he, a desire to end everything, including his life. She thought of their two young girls. What would she tell them? What would she tell everyone? It would destroy them all. They decided to move out of London. He swore he loved her, he needed her, he wanted to be with her, he didn't want to lose her or the children. If after that he gave in to his temptation – he said he didn't – she didn't know and she didn't want to know. If he did, he certainly was discreet. She wasn't, not with him, anyway.

Then there was an out of the blue 'hello' from her now married ex. He wrote to her old address. The letter, forwarded to her, was a few weeks out of date. She was surprised to learn he had long given up his get rich quick schemes and instead left for the US. He now taught anthropology at a prestigious college in Washington DC. She called the number he left. They were polite, friendly, nothing untoward was said or insinuated, and yet her heart raced as they spoke. He was coming to teach at SOAS in London for a semester. 'Would love to see you… If you are around.' They agreed to meet.

He was staying in a flat in central London, a street away from where she had once lived with her husband. He opened the door and smiled but she could tell he was just as apprehensive as she was. When he closed the door and tentatively entwined his fingers with hers, she melted. She didn't leave until the morning. Her husband knew she had taken a lover. Though he was deeply unsettled by it – she knew it broke his heart – he knew he had lost his rights as far as her love life was concerned. So, he kept quiet, just as she did about his secret longings. Her affair was a balm that soothed and healed and once again made her feel desirable and desired. When the seams came apart four months later as her Jamaican lover headed back to the States to his wife and his children, her husband was the one who helped Morayo stitch herself back up. It marked a turning point in their relationship. She discovered she loved her husband, as he loved her, in a way that eschewed logic. When he became ill, she was the one who, vehement in sparing his shame, told everyone, including the children, that it was cancer. And she kept up the lie, just as he had. Till death do us part, he whispered squeezing her hand a few days before he died. In the end, it was just him and her. She wept for her dead husband. But as she headed into the main kitchen to take the pepper soup off the Aga, she wept even more for herself, for all she had loved, for all she had lost.

A month later, Morayo prepared for what had quickly become a regular trip to Brixton. When her eldest daughter had rung –'*Mom*, I've been trying to call you, where have you been?'–her daughter's American twang was suddenly irritating. Her mother always commented on the pinched, narrowness of 'white' noses and how they all spoke as though their nostrils had been stuffed with groundnuts. Morayo imagined that her mother – who'd passed away while her grandchildren were still very young – would have had a giggle at how 'white' the girls sounded. Morayo was perturbed thinking how much that remark would have been laced with a secret sense of pride.

'What would you like me to do? Rot away in these four walls?!' Morayo wanted to yell at Charlotte. Truth was, aside from her trips to Brixton, Morayo rarely went out. Of course, she heard the phone. But conveying what she was feeling began to feel too uncomfortable, too complicated. What were the rules of grieving? She was sure she wasn't following them. It was easier to say nothing.

Today, Morayo decided to travel by train. She didn't need her car. On her last visit she had bought enough food to last a couple of months. On that trip, she had asked Bella to meet with her. Her daughter was a little puzzled. 'Mummy, why do you need to go to the market *again*?' Morayo's banter with the Asian man, something she had begun to look forward to, was watched by a silent Bella in part amusement and part suspicion. They drove back to the house together where she later watched Bella, enthusiastically, inquisitively, eating the *dodo* with jollof rice and stew she served and encouraged her to try. 'Gosh this is so good,' she said between mouthfuls. 'Why didn't you ever cook this when I was at home?' Her own child was eating and enjoying dodo! And jollof! And goat meat from the man in Atlantic Road! Morayo was overcome with emotion at the sight.

Today she was not shopping for food. She walked around Brixton, walking down the road opposite the park, where she, her parents and siblings had lived briefly. Ishes travelled the length of Coldharbour Lane, passing the boisterous locals blaring Shabba Ranks onto the streets. Schoolchildren chattered away melodiously, shirts carelessly sticking out, collars askew. An ageless Rastafarian riding his bike tooted his horn to greet strangers and friends alike. Noisy West Africans also passed Morayo by, their tones, gesticulations and laughs, even, all boldly projected. The familiar sounds of kissing teeth, the snapping of chewing gum, the concoction of languages and nuances lost in the English translation brought her a warmth she had not experienced in years. These were not scenes prevalent in the countryside.

Morayo suddenly felt tired. She then realized she had walked all the way to Camberwell Green. She got on a number 12 bus to take her into town so she could catch her train from Marylebone. The Routemaster was half empty when she got in.

'Good afternoon, Ma,' he tipped his hat politely to her. She sat in the four-seater, close to the conductor, immediately noticing his subtle but no less distinctive tribal marks. One on each cheek. Her father and his sisters had exactly the same. She looked at his badge. It was just a number, no name.

They talked about the weather, 'the children of today' and all those random but safe, well-versed topics of conversation strangers are generally united on. Every so often the bus would stop, passengers would board, and he would walk the length of the vehicle – including venturing upstairs – to collect fares and dish out tickets. Morayo could hear his brogue-covered feet coming down the stairs. He stood in the gap between the staircase and her seat and rang the bell.

'So, if you don't mind me asking, Ma, where are you from?'

'Oh,' she replied dismissively, 'I'm just here for the day, I live outside London.' He laughed 'No, no. I mean *where* are you from? Not *here*.' He made a face 'Which of us is really from here? We can't die here. This is not our country.' He narrowed his eyes, attempting to answer his own question' You don't quite look Jamaican to me...but I don't know, I could be wrong sha...' He raised his hand in a 'no offence' gesture.

'I am Nigerian.' Morayo's voice faltered slightly as the words came out. It was like trying to sing before warming up; her pitch was not quite right. She coughed and repeated herself. 'I am Nigerian.' This time when she found her voice it was strong, as if to convince not just the conductor but herself also.

'Eh, eh! Ah! Really?!' He was so surprised he was unaware he had lapsed into a heavier accent, removing his earlier formality. 'You don't sound it at all...your accent... You have been here a long time...'

It was not a question, but Morayo nodded her head anyway. She was unwilling to begin explaining that her birthplace was London, but she'd spent many of her childhood years in Lagos and Ibadan. And how does she put into words that even though she'd fallen in love and married a wonderful man, a man who gave her children anyone would happily boast about, a man who gave her a life so rich she would have been an ingrate to want for any more, a man many women would have prayed for, not knowing what they were wishing upon themselves, she had allowed herself to lose everything else in the process? No, she was not ready to explain. Not even to herself. And certainly not to a total stranger. This was not one of those *safe* conversation topics.

'I thought maybe you were from one of those small West Indian islands or something. So which state are you from?'

Morayo was glad they had reached her stop. 'My father is from Oyo State. Ibadan,' she said as she got off the bus. Turning round she noticed the happy shock on the face of the waving conductor as the bus drove away.

Not here. This is not our country. Long after Morayo arrived home, the conductor's words swirled around in her head. She looked out of the window at the trees and fields. She looked around the house as if for the first time. At the fireplace built from the repurposed stones that apparently once surrounded the walls of the town. At the Constable pictures on the wall owned by her husband's grandparents. At the grand Edwardian dining table and chairs surprisingly left to them by her husband's father. At the Chesterfield reupholstered in William Morris. At the Oscar Wilde, Chaucer and Tennyson first editions on the bookshelves. At the old bankers' lamps, at either side of the room, that had long stopped being in use. At the Aga which had now gone from cooking English roasts to frying dodo.

Morayo went into the bedroom. Hand-painted, bird-print wallpaper covered the walls from top to toe. The silk spread on the bed was also DeGournay. She pulled out her old telephone book and went to the phone. 'Yes, hello. Yes, I would like to book a flight to Lagos. No just one seat…. Let's check the end of the month… No…can I leave it open-ended? She smiled, nodding at the faceless voice beyond the receiver, her eyes shining with tears. 'Yes, I'm going home.'

UNDERNEATH THE MANGO TREE

The thick steam from the large pot she was carrying made her eyes dim to a squint, her nose rumple, her head recoil in caution. She took a couple of steps towards the doorless entrance before stopping to adjust the threadbare rag around her hands to stop her fingers from getting burnt again.

'Kemi! Kemi!!' She could hear her mother calling out impatiently from the back of the house. They had been preparing food since 5:00A.M. The laborious work that went into cracking, cleaning and grinding the melon seeds to make *egusi* stew, the cutting and cleaning of the goat meat, the peeling, the chopping and cooking of what seemed like endless pots of yam on wood fires... Kemi was exhausted and irritable. '*Mama, e nisuru!!!*' She failed to see the irony in loudly snapping back at Fehintola, her mother, to calm down and be patient as she carried the final pot to the backyard where she had been pounding freshly cooked blocks of yam into soft smooth mounds to be wrapped in banana leaves. An assortment of chattering local women were assisting to prepare the feast for the grand occasion. Fehintola sat, sweating from the heat and toil, legs splayed on a small wooden stool kept upright with cement blocks. She adjusted her wrapper to cover her modesty and rearranged her legs around the hefty wooden mortar. Without addressing her directly, she motioned for Kemi to place the steaming pot by her feet. *Thud, Thud, Thud.* The large wooden pestle hitting the yam, mixed with the salty sweat that dripped from Fehintola's forehead, *plop, plop, plop* became the rhythmic beat that peppered the brash voices of gossiping Yoruba women. The backing track was made up of young children playing raucously, the clucking of unkempt chickens, hawkers – dusty faced, shoeless boys and girls aged between six and seven – noisily proclaiming the goodness of their provisions and '*Sweet Like Victory!*' oranges that had been expertly peeled with a sharp razor blade. Like the other women, Kemi collected bricks from around the backyard which she used to create her own makeshift seat. The extension they had begun building was yet to be finished, so a good portion of the compound still resembled a cement factory. Draping an old cloth over the rough seat, she sat in front of the large frying pan of goat meat sizzling over a burning wood fire. Yawning crudely, she began to turn the meat over with a large wooden ladle. It felt like she had been awake forever. Mama Suleiman, a bubbly local woman that had been a friend of the family's for years, sympathized as she expertly tore *ewedu* leaves into the pot of ground melon seed stew. '*Pele*, Kemi.' Turning her gaze to the frying pan, she said, 'I know you're tired, but try to turn it quickly. You know if it is too black, it will be dry. We don't want it to bury itself in the middle of people's throats.' The rest of the women laughed loudly as Mama Suleiman over-dramatized her illustration of how the wedding guests would choke on the burnt meat. Kemi forced a small smile. It didn't reach her eyes. It was simply out of the respect expected and not because she found it particularly funny. The women always spoke to her as if she were a novice, as opposed to a grown woman with years of marriage behind her. And until she produced a living breathing child, she knew this would never change.

The women – with the exception of Ireti, the other wife of Kemi's polygamous father whose expression was a cross between nonchalance and restrained envy – launched excitedly into yet *another* conversation about the impending nuptials. Fehintola was happy to hold court for the purpose of fuelling Ireti's jealousy – repeating a story Kemi had heard about her younger sister's good fortune a thousand times.

'When Ronke brought him home, my eyes fell on him and my heart said, "This is the one". My sisters, o! Come and see the way he prostrated, the gifts! Money, foodstuffs, minerals! *Abi*, Kemi?' With shiny eyes, Fehintola stopped pounding for a second and looked to her eldest child to verify the legitimacy of her story. Kemi knew that even if Wale was one-legged with a face like an ape, as long as he came with crates of minerals – Fanta, 7UP, Coke, Malt – and pockets full of Naira and sterling, Fehintola would not have cared what her heart said. Kemi moved her head in a way that neither concurred nor disagreed. Her mother didn't seem to notice and simply carried on.

Hours later, the yard was left with the younger women. They had had their fill of gossip and were now drained of animation. Nobody had anything more to say. Tomorrow would be another day. Kemi's limbs ached as did her head. The requisite one-upmanship played out by her mother and Ireti over the years was tiresome. The only time Ireti and her mother had a remote sense of camaraderie was when their husband, Nisiru, married his third wife, the nubile, fair-skinned, Tinu Adamson. During that period, they were joint in a deep well of resentment, the walls of which were papered with their pain of rejection. Once that passed, Ireti and her mother carried on where they left off – bitter rivals masquerading as friends, fighting for the affections of a man who though still married to them, was no longer interested in the aged wives of his youth. It was a life that, even as a child, Kemi vowed never to have.

In the midst of clanging pots, Kemi could not help but compare the grand festivities taking place tomorrow with the preparations for her own wedding to Musa all those years ago. Ronke's dowry involved thousands of Naira, goats, chickens, (many slaughtered for the celebrations) yam, plantain, bags of gari and rice, crates of soft drinks and beer and, of course, the *aso-ebi* lace fabric from Switzerland and 24 carat gold jewellery from India. Her own dowry on the other hand could barely be quantified. This, claimed Fehintola, was justified as there were already rumours that Kemi had been seen about with '*that Hausa boy*', so 'which decent family will want to waste money paying for someone that has been soiled?' Even then, Kemi knew her mother was lying. She could not believe anyone would have known about her and Idris. They worked so hard at being discreet. They would go to places where they were sure familiar faces would be non-existent. It was in these places Idris would feed her stories about his life on his farm in Zaria and the life he led before his family moved down to the southern part of Nigeria.

She noticed him the first day he joined her school. The confident walk, sharp cheekbones and bright distrustful eyes that darted everywhere. He taught her to recite the *Surah Al-Fatiha*. She was so excited when she could eventually spout the sacred prayer off by heart. She knew her mother would be impressed. Ah, but she would also be suspicious. Yes, her family were Muslims, too, but they were not so staunch. So Kemi kept both the relationship and the recitation to herself. She told no one.

'Kemieeee!' She opened her eyes quickly. Lost in her thoughts, she hadn't heard one of the other women shouting her name. 'Kemi? Didn't you hear me calling you? Have you finished with the sponge?' As Kemi passed on the wire scrubber, she spotted her sister strolling leisurely towards the washing area. She automatically tensed and sighed heavily – enough for the lady next to her to inquire if she was okay. Kemi didn't have the opportunity to answer. The attention was no longer on her. *'Ah iyawo wa! Ronke, Iyawo!'* The women had begun regaling Ronke with wifely greetings and as she came closer, they broke into Ebenezer Obey's 'Eto Igbeyawo'.

'Eto igbe 'yawo l'aiye Oba Oluwa ni fi le ile, pelu ase ni. What God has joined together let no man put asunder,' they sang, tone-deaf in their broken English.

Ronke laughed girlishly as she demonstrated an elegant curtsy in front of the women. *'E ku se ma, E ma se gan. Olorun a se ti omo yin.'* She thanked them for all their hard work, proclaiming God would do the same for their own children. Kemi almost laughed aloud as she rinsed her final pot. Ronke had never been religious, but now that her fiancé was supposedly a fervent church goer, Ronke's thoughts on the matter had begun to sway. In public, at least. Before Wale, she would complain to anyone who cared to listen that 'Nigeria was using religion to indoctrinate people'. Yet, as she continued to pronounce blessings and favour over their households and families, the women loudly echoed their '*AMEEEEEENNN!!!!!!!*' as if they were being anointed by the Pope himself.

Kemi absorbed, not for the first time, her youngest sister's features. Smooth and unblemished, her fairness and fine features – the straight nose! – were always a talking point. Fehintola took pride in telling those that commented on her youngest daughter's beauty that Ronke had taken after her maternal great grandmother, a vain woman whose skin, judging by photographs and nostalgic stories, had not been blighted by the merciless African climate. As the engagement approached, their mother bought Ronke a *special* umbrella to keep her in the shade. 'Stay out of the sun. If you become black on your wedding day, people will think your husband has just married one illiterate from the North.' (An irony, considering Fehintola herself was barely literate.) She also authorized her to avoid 'any harsh work' in the run up to the nuptials. 'Every man wants a hard-working woman, but no man wants a woman with hands like a grater. I don't want Wale's mother to think her daughter-in-law has been working on a farm. She already thinks she is doing us a favour with that her oversized chin she likes to throw in the air.'

Kemi on the other hand, was already Black – she was the carbon copy of her paternal grandfather – so there was never any advice about keeping her hands soft or talk of special umbrellas. The day before her wedding, the biggest non-event of her life, she was still grinding tomatoes and pepper at the market for that evening's meal.

It was still dark outside; the cock was yet to crow but Kemi had no more sleep left inside her. She was right at the edge of the bed and shifted to face Musa. Her shoulder ended up on top of his chunky fingers. Adjusting her body to set his hand free whilst simultaneously moving the foot that dug into her calf muscle – she always told him he slept like a swatted fly – didn't wake him; Musa would have slept through Biafra. And even awake, there was not very much that moved him. Kemi stared at her husband. The moonlight shone on his skin, giving his blue-black face a silvery hue. His eyelids hid the eyes that Kemi could not help but pity. These were eyes she also resented. He was not particularly loving or tender, but he was a decent man. That, she couldn't deny. She was not aware of any philandering, which most of the other townsmen made no effort to be covert about. Seeing as the only thing she was pregnant with was shame, she was still surprised he had not found another woman. His mother, unusual for an African-in-law, did not put any pressure on them regarding children. She seemed to have accepted their fate; besides, Musa's siblings had provided her with grandchildren. Musa ignored his sisters who pleaded with him to take another wife. While he was not wealthy – he also had a limp, and evidently, as Kemi's mother so kindly put it, his face had not been favoured by the gods – his sisters still managed to line up a coterie of women who were happy to be his second wife and provide him with a much-needed heir. He always told his interfering sisters that 'a second wife only brings *"wahala"* into a man's home' and Musa enjoyed his peace. Kemi could never really understand why he was so loyal. She was grateful for his compassion but still, it could never be enough. He was not Idris. He could never be Idris.

She sometimes wondered what would happen if Idris ever came back to claim her. She knew that was never going to happen. Something her primary school teacher said once seemed apt. After they'd all finished reading the story of *Cinderella* she said, 'Children, these are what they call FAIRY TALES. Why? Because that is exactly what they are: TALES. Repeat after me FE-RI-TAY-ULS. These things do not happen in real life and if they happen, they only happen to white people. Not in Nigeria.' Kemi had accepted she would never see Idris again and no one else would have her heart. Thankfully, Musa never demanded that kind of love.

She thought she could make amends by giving him a child. It would also silence the ongoing talk of her barrenness. And for her, perhaps in some small way, it could compensate for losing Idris's baby. A loss she was forced to grieve for in secret. Kemi sighed as she sat up in bed, softly stroking her stomach. She did this almost automatically every morning after their night of what Musa referred to as 'sexsual relashons'. (She hated when he tried to speak English.) She would just lie there, immovable like a table, rarely making a sound. When she did, it would be to hoarsely scold her husband for squeezing her heavy breasts 'like someone who has just left prison'.

Kemi slipped her feet into her slippers and wrapped her Ankara cloth around her to cover her nakedness. She slapped a mosquito on her arm and walked out of the room, quietly closing the door behind her.

With the exception of three sounds – a very particular snore, the dull ticking of the old clock and the swirling fan, everywhere was still. It was 3:40A.M. In a few hours everywhere would be alive with wedding preparations. For now, it was still. The sitting room was a mass of unmoving bodies, lined up across the floor like sardines in a tin. In the night light, she recognized Mama Suleiman – she was the one who made the strangest noise, noticeably quivering as she slept. (Fehintola always said Mama Suleiman snored like she was being strangled.) Kemi almost lost her balance as she tried to avoid stepping on what looked like a child's hand. A number of relatives and family friends, all sleeping on mats laid out on the floor, had decided to stay at the last hour. She herself had no choice. Her mother had insisted – it was an obligation, not a request – she and Musa stay to 'support' her. A duty that had filled Kemi with dread.

As she closed the front door behind her, Kemi greedily breathed in the cool air, conscious that long before midday, everywhere would burn like an oven. Skin would blacken – not Ronke's of course – soles will burn and the stench of perspiration mixed with fried food would be ubiquitous. As she sat under the large mango tree at the corner of the Momodu compound, a subtle scent drove her nose upwards. The aroma was misleading. The fruit were still very small and although a hint of orange had begun to seep through the acid-green skin, for now, the texture of the normally ample fruit was wooden: the taste, unpalatably tart. The rainy season would begin in a couple of months. Then, the mangoes would flourish into glorious shades of gold, yellow, red and orange. At the height of the season, the soft, fleshy, overly ripe ones, scattered around the base of the tree, were usually eaten by children from around the neighbourhood. These were the mangoes that were no good to sell and too far gone to serve to important visitors. The children would eat and eat and eat till they were sick, their covetous eyes bigger than their small stomachs, while their mothers and grandmothers gossiped contentiously with Fehintola. It was under this tree she would secretly pick the best mangoes to give to Idris. It was under this tree she first felt the nausea of their child growing inside her. It was here she saw the trickle of blood running down her leg and knew immediately that the con-coction her mother had forced her to drink was having its way. It was under the mango tree she knew her first-born was dead.

Today was the day Ronke was getting married. For Kemi, however, it was the day after that held significance. Not today. For Kemi, tomorrow would be the beginning of the rest of her life. Because tomorrow, he was seeing the Babalawo. Tomorrow would be her final and most important visit.

For almost a year, Kemi had been visiting the Babalawo outside their district – the local one was far too indiscreet. It wasn't cheap and she had been saving some of the money from their household food shop. When Musa complained that the money he was giving her weekly didn't seem to be 'stretching' like before, she replied tartly, 'Can't you see aus-terity everywhere?' She also regularly cheated her mother when she worked in her store. She didn't feel guilty. *What price can be put on a life?* she would ask herself bitterly as she hid wads of Naira in her underwear. The cock crowed and Kemi became aware of the first light. She gently rose up from where she sat. Carefully re-tying her wrapper tautly around her body, she walked towards the house where she had already begun to hear the rumbling anticipation of an awoken household.

The wedding passed without incident. As expected, the guests gossiped and fawned over Ronke's good looks and even greater fortune. The food was excessive, so everyone ate until their faces – by now capitulated – resembled the inflated goats killed to celebrate Eid. Kemi even managed to dance to everyone's surprise. But unlike others, she was not dancing in ode to the newlyweds. Kemi knew, that as a family member, there was no way she would get up to dance without being sprayed with money by the more well-off guests. Of course, it was nowhere as much as her sister received but it was still substantial. As she remembered the Babalawo's prices, she held the notes to her forehead and swayed her hips even harder to the beat of the live band.

The next day after clearing up breakfast, she made her excuses, mumbling something about needing to drop by the tailor. Her mother, drowsy and exhausted from the previous day's affair and too tired to speak, acknowledged her with the wave of a hand.

Kemi hurriedly headed out before anyone could delve further into her exact whereabouts that day. Kemi could already feel beads of sweat forming across her fleshy chest. As she put her hand out to open the gate, she heard Musa calling her name with great urgency. She stopped, turned around slowly and noticed he was waving her purse in his hands. She had stuffed the wad of cash in her brassiere, so she had no need for her purse. Nevertheless, she smiled quickly as he handed it to her and carried on her way.

She took a taxi from the main road – she knew if she took the bus she was highly likely to bump into someone she knew. Kemi sat in silence. Even the bumping in and out of potholes and the tone-deaf driver singing to himself were not enough to pull her out her thoughts. As they reached the path that led to the witch doctor's house, she handed a wad of naira to him, stuffing the change of coins in her purse without checking to ensure she hadn't been deceived and climbed out the car She began to walk with a sense of urgency. Ten minutes later she was knocking on the door. By this time, she was already soaked with sweat, her mouth dry and her legs dusty from the uneven, sandy road. She was heady at the thought of what was to come – would she be allowed to shower first?

A well-dressed man in white shorts and a beige safari shirt opened the door. He was wearing strongly scented cologne and held a bottle of Sprite in his hand. He smiled widely, and it was only then that Kemi recognized the Babalawo

'How are you? Hope the family are well?' he asked cheerfully. He looked so different. Like an educated middle-class older man. Like the ones she sees on the rare occasions she goes to Lagos. 'Everybody is fine, thank you, *sa*,' Kemi replied nervously as she curtsied. 'Come in, come in and sit down, he said walking ahead of her and waving her into the house. 'I'll get my wife.' Kemi shut the door behind her and sat on the plush green-leather sofa. She looked at the photographs around the walls. In one, the man was dressed in a black suit and tie. In another, wearing a graduation gown. In a third, with his wife in matching lace. In another, his younger self with his wife and four children. They looked almost normal, thought Kemi. Although it was so commonplace to pay a visit to the witch doctor whenever you faced a challenge – whether that was another woman trying to steal your husband – or a middle child that was a dullard – for Kemi, this had been a new experience. When she saw the homes of witch doctors depicted on television, they never looked like this.

It was the wholesaler who sold Kemi toiletries for her mother's shop who'd passed on the witch doctor's details. She said Babalawo and his wife Iyanifa – no one knew their real names – she always greeted them as '*Ma*' and '*Sa*' – 'had divine powers. There is NO problem they can't find a solution to. They can do ANYTHING,' the wholesaler said.

At Kemi's last appointment, he and his wife were in full ritualistic regalia – headdresses, feathers, beaded belts, with matching black coal marks on their faces and hands. They prepared a concoction that would 'break the chains' around her womb. Through the Babalawo's consultation with the spirits, they had discovered her womb had been 'bound and shackled' by the family of her former lover – which is why she was not able to have children. For fifteen minutes after this revelation, Kemi was bound in a trance-like state as the couple chanted an intangible supernatural language while standing in the fresh blood of the bush rats they had killed earlier. The husband held black beads over Kemi's head while the wife rubbed her stomach with a pungent, dark, gritty substance. A moment of silence followed. Kemi sat up and was handed a small plastic bottle with a liquid the colour of urine. She was then told by the wife, 'Go home, drink this at midnight. What comes out of you afterwards, you must collect it, pour it into a gutter and watch it wash away. If you do not do this, exactly as I have told you, you and your womb will continue to be cursed.' Kemi was then told about the second part of the ritual, which would take place on her next and final appointment and would 'completely cleanse' her womb.

She was still staring at the walls of photographs when the wife walked in. Kemi stood up, 'Good morning, *Ma*,' she said curtseying as she did earlier. 'You are welcome,' replied the wife, beckoning Kemi to sit back down. She too, like her husband, was also dressed in casual, foreign clothes. Her head was covered with an ankara scarf which clashed somewhat with her English-style tea dress. She joined Kemi on the settee. 'Okay, so, did you bring the money?' the wife asked brusquely.

'Oh, yes of course,' answered Kemi, unnerved even more by her 'straight to business' tone. Kemi turned to the side and took out the tattered cloth in her brassiere. Unravelling it carefully, she gave the thick wad to the wife – the third, final and more substantial payment. The wife licked the tip of the second finger on her right hand and began to count with the expertise of someone used to handling great sums of cash. Satisfied, she stuffed the money into a side pocket and stood up abruptly. 'Okay, follow me. He is waiting for you.' She led Kemi to the kitchen, where a trapdoor lay flush to the floor in the middle of the room. With an assured tug, the wife lifted the door, and led Kemi down the steps into a tunnel. After navigating through a darkened maze, they finally came to a dark wood door. The wife rapped her knuckles on the door twice, and though there came no reply, nodded her head towards Kemi to proceed. Her face held no expression as she walked off briskly.

Kemi entered. The room was small and dark with only a dull flicker of light from a lantern in the corner. There was no evidence that the sun burned brightly outside. Though she knew to expect it, Kemi was still startled by the man lying on the bed, the only piece of furniture in the room. His arms were above his head, but she couldn't see his face clearly. She could hear his breathing. Soft and relaxed. It was contrary to hers, which she felt may have stopped. Kemi reminded herself why she was there and began to take off her clothes, her hands shaking. As she stepped towards the bed, the man spoke, his low gruff voice startling her.

'Close the door' Which would be the only words he'd utter to her. She went back to the door, did what she was told and came back to join the stranger on the bed.

The entire experience made her feel ashamed. She was pleased she didn't have to face the Babalawo and his wife afterwards – there was a back door she had been instructed to leave through. The shame continued to burn through her skin as she made her way back home. Her shame was not because she slept with a man that was not her husband – her desperation for a child, preferably a son, by any means necessary had curbed this. Her shame came from the acknowledgement that she enjoyed it far more than she knew she should have.

Over the next few weeks, she made sure, to Musa's surprise, to initiate their conjugal activities. He was happy to oblige, grateful for (and unsuspecting of?) his newly affectionate wife. Soon enough, the predictions of Babalawo and the wife came to bear. Kemi began to notice how the smell of *efo* and any kind of frying began to make her heave. Her breasts were tender; she was tired a lot and had developed a strange longing for the grit of cement on her tongue. And of course, her periods were nowhere in sight. Although she had not told Musa yet, she knew he had begun to notice her odd behaviour. More often than not, she'd catch him staring at her, an inscrutable expression on his face. Fehintola, on the other hand, seemed none the wiser. She had long relinquished any expectation of a grandchild, or anything else of note, from her eldest daughter.

They had retired to their room for the night when Musa suddenly asked, 'So when are you going to tell me what is happening with you?' She turned to him and laughed quietly, as she rubbed her stomach. 'I was wondering when you were going to say something. At last,' she paused and then continued. 'God has blessed us with a child.' She could not understand why Musa's face fell. She dropped her smile. 'What is the problem, Musa? Is this not what everybody has been waiting for? Is this not what the whole town has been using to taunt me all these years? You think I don't know what they say behind my back?' Kemi knew she had begun to sound defensive.

Musa looked her straight in the eye and said 'Kemi, what have you done? You think I'm a fool? We both know this child does not belong to me.' Kemi's mouth dried up and she lost her ability to speak. The wave of nausea that came over her was totally unrelated to her pregnancy. Musa's broken voice sounded like it was coming from afar. 'I know I cannot have children.' He paused looking at his wife as if expecting her to have an answer. Too shocked to respond, Kemi looked on, her eyes terrified. He turned away and continued. 'Your mother knew this before we married. She said it did not matter. She said that after what happened to you…she said you no longer could have children anyway, so…' Kemi began to wretch so fiercely her sick turned from a bright green to a deep brown. Musa looked on impassively, before saying quietly 'I don't know where you got this pregnancy from. You better decide what you are going to do with it.' With that, he left the room, gently closing the door behind him.

WAIT

A few weeks ago, when your mother came to see the baby, she told me she saw Ngozi on the Hammersmith & City Line. When she added 'She's just here for summer,' I felt a little less anxious. I did hear quite some time ago that Ngozi had left the country; apparently, she now lives in Atlanta. I also heard that she completely left the faith. This didn't surprise me. I doubt it is surprising to you. Your mother seemed shocked. Particularly when she was describing Ngozi's new piercings while she was trying to rock the baby to sleep.

'Come and see!' she said, her eyes wide. 'Not just the ears, o! Nose, eyebrow, lips, even the tongue! *Haba*! Where are her parents? Such a pretty girl. Why would she spoil her face like that?' It was rhetorical of course so I didn't answer. Then she whispered that Ngozi was holding hands with someone: 'A woman! Can you imagine? She left church and this detty business is now what she is doing with her life?!'

Your mother was trying to drag me into a conversation I didn't really want to have. Maybe she noticed I wasn't taking the bait, so she switched to how we all need to pray for Ngozi so that, 'the eyes of her understanding become enlightened'. I just said, 'Amen, *ma*' and kept my face straight as I lifted our sleeping child from her arms and laid her in the cot. The purpose of your mother's visit was to help with the baby, but her words have left me even more anxious and sleep deprived. I'm now wondering who else she has shared that story with, who else has heard? Did she say anything to you? It's not the first time I've wondered if you had heard something or knew something. In fact, there have been many times over the years when I wondered if you ever suspected. Then I would ask myself whether it mattered. Was it still relevant? Even now? Also, how much are we supposed to share with the person we are married to? Everything? And how far back does one go? I didn't have concrete answers so I would go back to trying to keep my questioning mind quiet. I still don't have the answers, but after that conversation with your mother, it might be time to no longer stay silent. When you are told to wait, made to wait, forced to wait, sometimes things happen that leave you with baggage long after the wait is over. These are things I can no longer hold on to.

Do you remember what happened on the day we got back from exchanging our vows? I hid. You didn't know I was hiding but that's what I was doing when I shut myself in the toilet downstairs. You knocked, tentatively, concerned and I responded that I felt a little unwell.

'Ah,' I heard you say impassionedly. 'You are healed in Jesus's name.' I sensed you were trying to iron the crease of disappointment in your voice; the dismay that we, potentially, would have to delay our consummation for yet another day. For every Christian couple schooled in the morality of denying oneself, the idea of waiting, of abstaining for one more day, when you were now legitimately allowed to have sex, was one day too many.

'Yes, I'm sure I'll be fine,' I injected a faux lightness into my voice which I hoped obliterated the deadness I felt. I refused to scratch the itch that threatened to fire back meanly at your religious optimism. No, I'm not criticizing you. If anything, I secretly admired it, desired it even; this unquestionable faith you had, probably from the start. It was one, unlike mine, that was unlikely to be blemished with ungodly thoughts and earthly doubts.

Which is why as I sat on the floor, one hand on my head, the other holding the side of my ribcage tight, trying to breathe. The toilet was painted white in order to bring in as much light as possible. But I sat there descending into darkness wondering what on Earth I'd just done.

I have no idea when the world began to tell me to dream about my own wedding. Was it at birth, when my parents subliminally projected their own dreams onto the six-pounder screaming before them? Or was it when the pretty, subservient dolls I was gifted as a young girl began to feel incomplete unless they had a man at their side? Or was it much later, when smug married couples in church looked upon your singleness as an illness that had the terrifying potential to be terminal? It didn't matter that you were degree educated, that you had a decent, if nascent career, that you weren't related to Quasimodo, that you had all your teeth. If you were a single woman in church, you may as well be a leper. I know you think I'm exaggerating, but ask any single woman in church and she will tell you the same thing: singledom is like a curse we are tasked with breaking. And so, we were encouraged to 'serve' at church. We were told, when you serve, 'like Ruth, your Boaz will find you. So let your husband find you serving...' (For a while I actually joined the church ushering team. I made sure my permanent smile gleamed with zeal. Until it didn't. I still didn't meet anyone. Until you – and you didn't meet me serving.)

At the singles meetings, we were constantly reminded by church elders – who had been having sex for years – how important it was to keep yourself pure, regardless of how hard and fast and constant your desires pulsated. The annual singles conference was always heaving, mainly with women, their pores emitting the scent of desperation. They lifted their voices in one accord to pray against the spirit of singleness and asked for the Lord that neither slumbered nor slept to hurry up and bring their husbands. I was once one of those women. Yes, even when the true realities of 'marriage' stared me dead in the face. For many years, my mother left home every weekday morning at 4:00A.M. to clean offices. She squirrelled a lot of her wages away to build a small house in Ikorodu on the outskirts of Lagos. Her social-security benefits on the other hand went towards the upkeep of my brothers, because as you know, my father spent most of his time and money on women who were not his wife. Nevertheless, I looked past all of the lies and infidelities, and devoured dreams of my wedding whole. Because of course my own life was *not* going to be like that.

I dreamt about the *aso-oke* I would wear – dark purple with a pink *gele* – with an excessively bejewelled fuchsia shoe-and-bag set my mother and I would buy in one of the Italian shops off Petticoat Lane market.

I dreamt how I would dance. So exquisitely, that you, my husband would look on in wonder. And then my in-laws would join you in spraying me with enough money to drown in.

I dreamt that my wedding would be in London – not Nigeria – because I didn't want a thousand guests, most of whom I would never have invited but my parents and your parents would have insisted on. They would have said 'But ah, how can we not invite them? They were very good to us in the sixties. Don't you remember my grandfather's third wife's brother in law's daughter's stepsister? Of course we have to invite the church members. We are Africans, this is what we do...' I also didn't want my wedding in Nigeria because I didn't want the heat to frizz the ends of my hair or melt my mascara into my eyes.

I dreamt about the extensive but slightly unorthodox menu. There would be everything from jollof and fried rice to *moi moi* and Nigerian salad – which of course isn't really a salad at all because normal people don't add things like corn beef or green peas or copious amounts of Hellman's to a normal salad. There would also be paella which, yes, is odd at a Nigerian wedding, but from the first time we made it in Home Economics, I always thought it would go well with an assorted meat stew. The aunties would all smirk, but I would dig my heels in.

I dreamt of a six-tiered Victoria Sponge. (I never wanted the requisite fruit cake. But in reality, I had to concede, as fruit cake was *your* favourite). The guests would indulge in everything without restraint. I of course would barely put anything past my lips, as my excitement and fervour for my new husband would be so overwhelming it would steal my appetite. Except it didn't. I did eat. But I only did it as a way to suffocate the small insistent voice that kept saying, 'He's not the one. He's not the one. He's not the one.' It was her voice. These are things I never told you.

I met Ngozi at a women's singles conference. There was a main speaker, I can't remember her name now. But I do remember her powder-pink skirt suit with a flower brooch on the lapel, her cream tights and her poofy hair. I remember her telling the audience that she had flown in 'alllllll the way from Houston, Texas!' The crowd responded in such an excited and inane way (all the *wooooos* began to hurt my ears), as if she had walked all the way to the North London venue from Neptune. Her sermon took us back ten years to a time when she was twenty-six. ('Gurl, thirty was gonna be knocking on my door in a hot minute!' she said with horror. Everyone laughed nervously.) It was a 'dark time' when she was a wretched, desperate being like the rest of us, who were now hanging on to her every word in the hope that by God's grace we could overcome the secret terror of going past our sell-by dates. It was during this 'dark time' that she 'sought the Lord' and received a deep, spiritual insight into how to 'wait with purpose'. Voilà. Before long, she was 'found' and is now smugly married to the 'best man on earth; my king, my God-given man, my everything'. She had a gargantuan diamond ring or two. She also said that, even after quite a few years of marriage, they had a hot but Godly sex life ('We keep it Godly, ladies, we keep it Godly'). It was sex without the fear of illegitimate pregnancies, sex without being gossiped about in church and sex without spending a lifetime in the throes of Satan and chlamydia. If we bought her book *The Wait* – it would, she promised, reveal how to wait for our husbands because if it was done properly, 'he will be right on time, and it will be right! Amen, ladies?!'

For an extra ten pounds she signed the book. Because of course her scrawl is exactly what we needed to give us an extra dose of holiness while waiting for our husbands. Sorry, yes, forgive me, I am being facetious. I'm also tired. In so many ways.

After her talk, I waited in the queue, yawning and moving my weight impatiently from one foot to the other to buy *The Wait*. And no, the irony was not lost on me.

'Are you already tired of waiting for *The Wait*? How will you be found by your husband?' I suddenly heard behind me. I was curious to know who was responsible for this brazen gravelly voiced irreverence. And the scent of Dior's *Poison*. (I immediately recognized it because I'd smelt it – and loved it – at a department-store counter in Central London. My mother, who was with me at the time, said, 'Yewande, do you think God wants you to wear a perfume called *Poison*?' So, she bought me Estée Lauder's *Beautiful* instead.)

I turned my head to see a slim, athletic looking, light-skinned woman. Physically, she was the complete opposite to me; a dark skinned, unmistakably African looking woman who couldn't remember a time she didn't struggle with her weight. The only thing we seemed to have in common was that we were, from my rough guesstimation, around the same age. Her hair was pulled back into a slick ponytail making her feline eyes and robust, pink lips the centre of attention. She barely wore make-up (I on the other hand never left home without foundation or lipstick). She was striking. I didn't understand why she joined the queue for *The Wait*. Why was she even at a women's singles conference? Why would a girl that looked like her still be single? (Much later down the line, I remember you saying that her mouth was 'very sharp' and probably 'too much *wahala* for any man to deal with'.)

In the months that followed, Ngozi left her church – which she said she only really attended sporadically – and joined ours. (You, of course, didn't know any of us then – it was also just after you had left to attend Bible School in Florida.) Suddenly, attending church was fun. She was the irreverent, confident, dry-humoured sister I never had. Growing up with boys, it felt novel but also familiar; she was deliciously ungirly. In church terms, certainly. All the other church girls, girls like me, had become almost crazily consumed with waiting to be found. Ngozi on the other hand was totally carefree about the wait. She never really talked about that. I would love to say she inspired me to cast aside this pressing desire to relinquish my singleness. She didn't; the end goal of the wait was too deeply ingrained. But she did provide a certain lucidity, a pause, like an interval at the opera, and for that I was grateful. Grateful also for the way she gave life to thoughts the rest of us never dared to voice. Like when the assistant pastor announced that everyone needed to start giving an even bigger 'sacrificial offering' during service. We had, just the month before, given another 'sacrificial offering' for new church buses. This time it was to go towards a full church-renovation plan. There was talk of fancy American-style interiors, swish new carpets and chandeliers handmade in Italy. Ngozi openly said she wasn't contributing to it. 'If his faith is that strong for overpriced lighting, let him believe God for it,' she said grumpily. Some mouths twisted in disapproval, but I also spotted eyes filling with awe. On another occasion I told her that your mother pulled me aside to say my knee-length skirt was 'too tight and distracting' for church 'and life in general'. When I told her this, Ngozi rolled her eyes and said, 'First Lady needs to focus on her daughter's inability to keep her underwear on.' Which was true. Everyone knew about Toyosi's looseness. I'm sorry. I'm really not trying to be rude. I know your sister has settled down now… If it helps, the general consensus was that a pastor's daughter going off the rails was almost a rite of passage.

Every Sunday after church I went to Ngozi's large flat in Central London, which she shared with two non-Christian friends (another thing looked on disapprovingly by many of the church girls, especially because one of the housemates was a boy). This particular Sunday, she had stayed home to study; she was in the middle of her master's, which her wealthy parents back in Nigeria were paying for. ('My mother and father only have bachelor's degrees. So, they live vicariously through me,' she once deadpanned). I slipped out of church just before the end of service to see her. She had prepared lunch: scrambled eggs with peppers, tomatoes, onions and herbs to go alongside sweet, deep fried yam chunks and Supermalt. As we ate, Ngozi, still in her negligee and dressing gown, bitterly complained about yet another man in church who was in pursuit of her. Just one in a long line of potentials desperate to date her. 'At least you have *someone* interested in you,' I said.

She raised her head from her plate, put her cutlery down and looked me dead in the eyes. She didn't flinch and I suddenly began to feel nervous, my heart racing so hard and fast and loud I was sure she could hear it. Ngozi slid her hand into mine and said quietly, 'I'm not interested in him. I'm not interested in any of them.'

There's no point in talking about all the things that happened between Ngozi and I in the two years that followed. There was the thrill of the risk and the excitement of the new but if it makes you feel any better, it was mingled with a dense fear, shame and self-loathing. It was so confusing. One minute I felt freedom. And then not. It kept me awake at night. (You've asked when and how my insomnia began. Well, now you know.) I felt like I was in the clutches of something that I just couldn't detangle myself from. Anytime I came up for air, I was smothered once again. Strangely, even in my stupor, something in me knew. I knew there was no hope, no life, no future, no point in what we were doing. For me, it always had a shelf life. Ngozi, on the other hand, surprised me with her delusion about our future together. We once had a blazing argument because she was so offended when I said something about still waiting for my husband. Her own plans were centred around our escape route, where we could go, where we would live, where we could run to. I have had many doubts over the years – over my life, my choices, my faith – but if there's one thing I was always sure of was that living openly – or in secret - with a woman was not part of the life I envisaged for myself. This wasn't a fight I was willing to take on. This wasn't part of the dream I'd been taught to dream. And when it came down to it, I was not prepared to sacrifice the dream I had waited for and spent so long – whether knowingly or subconsciously – cultivating. But I didn't know how to stop this, this... *thing*, with Ngozi. So, when you came back from America, when you noticed me, when you, the Pastor's son, chose me out of the sea of waiting girls that in my mind were probably better suited for you, it was the get out clause I needed. It was validated when you finally said the words that I needed to hear, that you believed I was the one for you. I saw it as a sign, perhaps of God trying to save me from myself. I deceived myself thinking Ngozi and I could still be friends, but we lapsed into stolen moments that always ended up being fraught. She was so envious; I was so torn. The night you presented the ring, I decided I had to finally make a choice. I was at Ngozi's flat one winter's night for the very last Sunday. She was broken. She wept, pleading with me to change my mind. I didn't want to lose her but there was no other way. I had to. There was, of course, a part of me that was scared she would expose me, but I also knew she had a lot to lose, too – she wasn't ready to come out. Not then, anyway. Eventually I began to feel exhaustion from the hours of trying to explain what I didn't really have the words to. 'He's not the one. He's not the one,' she kept saying hysterically. Finally, I screamed: Stop it! How do you know that? What do you know? Oh, are you suddenly an expert on men?!' It was cruel, I was cruel. By then, I couldn't think or see straight, my own tears had formed steamed shields over my eyes and my brain was a pool of chaos. I left barely conscious of where I was headed.

Now you know the real reason Ngozi left church, why I never heard from her again.

Until she called me yesterday. Yes, Ngozi called me. She had changed her number, but I hadn't changed mine. I almost dropped the baby when I heard the voice at the other end.

Our conversation was pleasant, surface level and thankfully short. I don't remember much of it – I was in a daze.

'I'm still here for the next few weeks... I'd love to see you,' she said and those words stayed with me. I have not stopped thinking about her; not in the way you think, though. I have no desire to see her, to rekindle our...whatever it was. Or anything else. But what I was reminded of, was that in the end, at least she was honest about who she was and what she wanted. And she was bold enough to follow after it, damn the consequences. I, on the other hand, have not been honest. I have spent our marriage not being honest to you or me. The day you told me that you loved me and I told you I loved you, I lied. I didn't really love you. But I don't know if I knew that then. In the years that followed, I realized that what I actually loved was the dream I'd been fed. I didn't feel the heavy flutter of butterflies the world had said I would feel in the genesis of our dalliance, I didn't think about you every waking minute, I didn't feel lost without you. I didn't feel distracted by my feelings for you. I didn't feel like I couldn't go on without you. Now, this isn't about Ngozi. I don't want to diminish what I had with her and call it a moment of madness, though I'm sure many will. For me, it was simply a moment. A thrilling and sometimes terrifying moment. Nothing more. I was curious; I satisfied my curiosity. That was that. Think about it: in the end, I didn't choose Ngozi. But if I'm being totally honest,

I didn't choose you, either; I chose the dream. I loved the dream of what was promised at the end of the wait. But it didn't love me back. Which is why, when we arrived home after our wedding, I felt so hollow. I thought, at some point, like a fog, it would begin to lift, and the season would pass. One day I hinted as much to my mother. Without looking up, she said quietly, 'Do you think I was in love with your father when I married him? Sometimes you have to wait for these things to grow. And sometimes they don't. You just have to find your joy elsewhere. You can't eat love.' But my life was never going to be like hers, remember?

So, I still held onto the hope that my lingering emptiness would fade and develop into something quite extraordinary. The kind of thing where when I think of you, something inside me constricts and I need to gasp for air. The thing where I have a deep, constant desire to bury my head in your neck and leave me there forever. The thing where, when we fight, my love for you still manages to burn much deeper than my anger ever could. The thing where my longing for you is so gloriously intense it comes with an acute sense of pain. The thing where, when you burn through me with your eyes, my body begins to melt and every part of me gets hot with desire. Are all these ridiculous things signs of being in love? What would I know? All I know is that seven years of marriage hasn't cleared the fog. Which is why I want to start afresh. On my own. I want to go back to the wait but not like it was before. This time I want to decide on the rules of the wait. I don't want to wait in the way I was taught to wait. I don't want to wait for what I was conditioned to wait for. I just want to wait for love. Whatever that is.

TRIP

Unlike most fourteen-year-olds, Lara was an experienced funeral goer. Most of the dead were not people she really knew, but in her town, funerals were open invitations where you could watch human behaviour from a safe, inconspicuous distance. They were also social moments where you saw other stragglers you perhaps had not seen since the last funeral. And for Lara and her young friends, it was also a great opportunity to eat copious amounts of jollof rice and fried chicken necks for free. The truly bereaved, she was sure, had little appetite for food.

She had watched, dry-eyed but equally fascinated and terrified, as mourners wailed, weeping hysterically, rolling in the dust with fervour, renting their clothes with such determination it brought to mind biblical times. And Nollywood films. This funeral was different.

Though she knew that she didn't have it in her to scream 'take me with you' while throwing herself on the coffin as it was being lowered, she knew it was important, necessary, in fact, to cry. And yet, it was as if something heavy and unyielding sat on her tear ducts. Perhaps she was in shock. Perhaps she had internalized her grief. Perhaps she was in denial. Whatever the case, she knew no excuse would be an excuse. That she didn't cry would be seen as demonic.

Lara needed a trigger. Which is why she asked to see the body one more time. The elders were surprised at her insistence, this was not the norm by any means. After failing to dissuade her, they finally acquiesced: two men – she assumed from the funeral home – undid the latches and pushed the lid open.

Lara didn't recognize her own mother. Her hair, usually hidden in braids under a scarf, was left to fill out the top of the casket like a static Medusa. Thick and wiry, the fine streaks of white looked like they had been brush stroked for the occasion. Her attire – a white lace dress festooned with teeny diamante studs – was quite possibly the most expensive she had ever seen her mother wear while she was living. Lara was intrigued by the matching tufts of cotton wool jammed in her nose, in her mouth, in her ears. She felt compelled to reach out and touch her face. Her mother's skin did not feel at all like skin. Rather, it was perfectly, solidly cold.

It was then that she broke down. Considering the detachment she had long felt towards her mother, who had been consumed by a depression that refused to leave after Lara was born, she was surprised at how raw, genuine and heartfelt her grief was. The wash of tears wouldn't stop. She began to wail.

Someone held her close – she wasn't quite sure who, but whoever it was smelt like overripe bananas and mothballs – and led Lara back to her seat. Over her shoulder, she took a last, fleeting look at her mother from the corner of her eye as the coffin was closed again… For someone who lived her life with a permanently stony expression, her features, while thoroughly ravaged by cancer, were softer than Lara had ever seen them.

Even as early as 5:00A.M., the stiff, African heat was unyielding. The journey on the way to the airport in Brother Biko's old rusty danfo was clothed in apprehension – there were no shortage of stories in their town of all the bad things that could possibly happen on the day people travel – anything from missing your flight to having a car accident. One had to stay solemn and prayerful. Lara's light attempt to shift the mood with conversation was greeted with non-committal nods and monosyllabic responses, eventually forcing her to keep her thoughts to herself. In between fiddling with her sacred beads and softly muttering under her breath, her grandmother, Mama Wura, wrung her hands, as she tended to do whenever she was contemplating bad news.

The three passengers – Brother Biko at the wheel, Mama Wura in the passenger seat and Lara sitting behind her – hit the inevitable traffic at the frenzied Illupeju market. What would normally be a bother became a welcome distraction for Lara. Anything but the silence. A barrage of car horns sounded all around them. Large troops of colour-coded children – red pinafores with white collars, blue and white check dresses, green shorts with khaki-colored shorts – garrulously marched along to their respective schools. The boys had the clean lines of newly barbered hair while the girls' neat, tight cornrows looked fresh from the weekend. Their teeth shone white like the flesh from a broken coconut and their faces gleamed like they had been marinated in vegetable oil. As if playing a game of which she was the only contender, Lara softly read the words inscribed on the kaleidoscopic melee of bags which flew past their van. 'ILLUPEJU PRIMARY SCHOOL... BARUGA GRAMMAR SCHOOL... LADY OF OUR CROSS SCHOOL... IFE OLUWA NURSERY AND PRIMARY SCHOOL... TO GOD BE THE GLORY...'

Lara stopped reading. Seeing the schoolbags was a reminder of the classmates she would be leaving behind. She felt like an ingrate. She knew she was very fortunate to be going to live in London. She had been told that by everyone who knew she was leaving to live with her 'rich Aunty'. But still, there was so much, from the dramatic to the prosaic, that she was sure she would miss in Lagos. She noticed the market women setting up their fruit and vegetable stalls– it was pawpaw season, they were everywhere – their crying babies tightly tied to their backs with faded wrappers of cloth. The lucky few opened sun umbrellas to shield them from the oppressive light of day, some so dirty it was difficult to establish their original colour. The vendors all chattered loudly and enthusiastically, their voices competing with the cacophony of sounds found throughout the market.

A few feet away, a cluster of emaciated chickens squawked loudly while pecking away at old food remnants left over from the previous day's trading. A man in a white singlet and khaki shorts walked past briskly, balancing an old sewing machine on his left shoulder, his rubber slippers slapping the back of his hardened heels. On the other side of the road, Lara watched an ageing man baring his protruding stomach atop a pair of loose blue and yellow tie-dye cotton trousers. He stood over the gutter as he brutally brushed his teeth with a fresh yellow chewing stick. He seemed impervious to the putrid stench from the overfilled sewers – a mix of general waste and spoiled produce grudgingly thrown away by the sellers. Food rotted by the merciless heat. He spat out the contents of his mouth, straw-like sticks flying everywhere, and used the remainder of his water to rinse his face. Barefooted hawkers traded their wares coarsely, slapping the palm of their hands on the van to attain business.

'Bread-io! Bread-io! Bai your bread! Bread-io! Bai your bread!' The aroma of warm, freshly baked bread wafted up her nostrils and made her mouth water. She locked eyes with the hawker – a young girl with pinched features and two large tribal marks across both cheeks. Lara now regretted the large bowl of *ogi* she had drunk for breakfast that morning. Her body felt like it wanted to expel the thick white, mucuslike liquid and replace it with the more solid loaf. As if by intuition, the girl began to unload the tray of hot loaves from the top of the twisted and knotted Ankara cloth she used to balance the foodstuffs on her head.

'Aunty, look.' She shoved the tray as far into Mama Wura's window as she could. 'Fresh bread. Small one: fifty kobo. Big one: one Naira. Aunty buy it, buy it now. Fresh bread.'

Mama Wura waved the girl away like someone shooing away a diseased cat. The girl ignored Mama Wura and carried on, her little legs swiftly moving to keep up every time the car edged forward in the notorious Mushin 'go-slow'. '*Ewo*, bread *yi fine gan*. Aunty, *e ra* bread, o fine *gan*. Bred-io. Bread.' The girl tried to plead for them to buy her 'fine' stock, her gaze lifeless, preprogrammed to give a buoyant sales pitch but with eyes that refuse to line up. Mama Wura now lost her patience and raised her voice. 'We don't want it! Are you deaf?' she said brusquely in Yoruba. 'Take your things and go!'

Lara looked down embarrassed, discreetly making a face. The car suddenly began moving faster – there had been a let up in the traffic – and the hawker girl had to hastily grab a tighter hold of her tray and step back as the car began to speed away. As if carried by the wind, the girl's '*Ko ni da fun yin!*' resounded in the car. With the exception of the oblivious Brother Biko, one of their neighbours who offered to drive them, who still kept his eyes firmly on the road, they were visibly stunned by the ease at which the girl was able to hurl abuse at an elder without fear of the malediction that tradition says she would bring on her future.

'*Oloshi*. It's her father's father she's talking to.' Mama Wura quietly returned the girl's curse that life will never be well with her, confident that though she was long gone, the imprecation would catch up with her one way or another. Mama Wura went back to wringing her hands. The rest of the journey was spent in silence.

Flanked by her forlorn-looking grandmother and Brother Biko, Lara arrived at an unconditioned Murtala Muhammed Airport and an already heat-weary crowd who, with their various languages, dialects, pitches, tones and gesticulation, produced a spectacle that could be likened to the confusion at Babel. At this point, Lara thought, perhaps she wouldn't miss life in Nigeria after all.

'Isn't that the British Caledonian desk there?' Brother Biko's earlier slumber had begun to ebb away. He pointed to a disorganized mass of human beings a few yards away, the airline emblem lit brightly above their heads. Although he spoke in Yoruba, his deliberate intonation of 'British Caledonian' betrayed his pride at being able to say those words, almost as if he had been practicing, desperate for the opportunity to say it publicly.

'*Oya, Oya, e je ka lo. E niso,*' Mama Wura urged, hurrying them to move toward the intimidating looking crowd. Biko dragged along Lara's bulging suitcase while she gripped her equally stuffed hand luggage – an old dark blue polyester carry-all with wine coloured piping. It had a patch on the front that read 'MAYFLOWER GIRLS'. Her mother had bought it years ago in the used-clothing market. It was the school all the local girls aspired to attend, but of course, Mama Wura would have never been able to afford the fees.

They approached the chaos at the British Caledonian desk. In what was an unorthodox but typically Nigerian version of a queue, the mass was jumbled, exodus-like in the midst of heaving suitcases, bags and cardboard boxes, languidly waiting for the desk to open: A heavily made-up young woman, surrounded by her equally made-up friends of typical *sisi eko* – single Lagos girls – chattered excitedly about their friend's trip to London; An Igbo family was noisily disagreeing on how to repack their overstuffed luggage to avoid paying excess; A bare-chested little boy, with a terrible case of heat rash and a runny nose, complaining of thirst to his neatly dressed mother. She fanned him with the lid of a plastic container while trying to appease him with the promise of 'soon'; and a man dressed in a grey damask, traditional shirt and trousers sat on his mat with a newspaper to keep him cool. A dark wet patch under his right arm became visible every time he adjusted his makeshift fan to combat the taut heat. An orange flask, tin of Carnation milk and a large plastic mug at his side, indicated he had either arrived at an ungodly hour or stayed in the airport overnight.

Suddenly and without warning an attendant appeared at the desk, signifying the start of the check-in procedure. The crowd abruptly stood to attention and messily surged forward to take their place in the puzzling, queue system. The beginnings of an argument arose between a stern, impatient young woman sporting a short no-nonsense afro and a rotund, dark-skinned woman in her late forties, her skin aglow with sweat. To everyone's annoyance, the older lady's excessive luggage, splayed all over the floor, slowed down the exodus. The crowd began to grumble loudly – a superfluity of accents, languages, high- and low-pitched voices from a weary, irritable and overheated mass. Mama Wura couldn't quite understand what was happening, but she knew it was not good. As she began to prophesy the end – '*O pari!*' – a firm, authoritative voice rose from somewhere in the crowd.

'Can one of the gentlemen just join me and help the lady with her bags so we can speed things up?' Lara began to look around, along with the majority of the throng, to see who had spoken. A regal-looking, dark-skinned man sporting a blue suit and hair like thick, black cotton wool made his way through the crowd. Lara expected the awestruck people to touch the hem of his garment as he passed. The man moved with such ease and clout that the crowd parted, and their grumblings faded to a hush. A few of the other men – including Biko – eagerly rushed forward to do as he had suggested. To Mama Wura's relief – the unfamiliar surroundings of the airport were making her nervous as it was – the rest of the check-in process passed without incident.

Later, filled with fish pie and fizzy drinks, they headed towards the departure gate.

In less than eight hours Lara would be in London. It was where she was to begin her new life with Aunty Ronke and her husband Wale (ever since his graduate stint at Lagos University Teaching Hospital, everyone called him Doctor). Lara was too young to remember them – the couple had left the year Lara was born, had returned to visit soon after but never since. All Lara saw of them were the old pictures from their wedding day. Doctor, said at the time to be one of the most eligible men in town, was picture-book hand-some. Aunty Ronke was exactly the kind of woman you could imagine a man like him would end up with. She was light-skinned, curvy –with a small waist – and her facial features were symmetrical and girlish, her hair relaxed straight, the dark wavy extensions providing an enviable length and added fullness. She looked stunning. Still, Mama Wura would always say with pride, 'Not even the best photographer can capture Ronke's beauty.' When once, a distant elderly relative remarked that while the couple were living a successful life in London, it's a shame they didn't come 'home' more often', Mama Wura responded irritably. 'Baba, my daughter is living the good life in London. Her husband is now a big medical doctor working in one of London's best hospitals. Their children are going to very good schools. But you want them to come back? For what? For the mosquitoes? For all the jealous eyes to be eyeing them? For them to be living under this useless government that has eaten all our money, so we don't have good electricity or good roads. What are they coming back for?'

It was time to go through departures. Lara's grandmother gave her a final farewell. '*Oya niso, bami ki Ronke ati ara ile. Se dada. Ma di oloshi ni* London *o.*' Lara almost burst out laughing. She had watched so many American films where airport farewell scenes were wrapped up in high emotion and endless tears. This moment felt so far removed from that. Her grandmother had simply sent greetings to Ronke and her household and warned Lara not to become an idiot in London. At this point, however, Lara appreciated Mama Wura's sharpness. With so many changes afoot, her grandmother's consistency was calming. Stifling a chuckle, Lara answered 'Yes, Ma' politely. Mama Wura embraced her granddaughter, again beckoning her to hurry to avoid missing her flight. Brother Biko stepped forward to give Lara a firm pat on the back, reminding her not to forget her family, like most Nigerians do once abroad. She was glad he didn't try to hug her; his body odour already threatened to decimate her. As she went through the gate, Lara turned to give one last wave. She was surprised to see Mama Wura using the corner of her wrapper to roughly dab the corners of her damp eyes.

Despite her nerves, Lara slept better on the flight than she had in the last month. Perhaps she had subconsciously cast her cares away as the plane flew across the Atlantic. Nigeria was behind her and a new life awaited.

By the time they landed at London Heathrow six hours later, she was excited at the prospect of starting afresh. After disembarking, she followed the signs and the crowd towards where she assumed she would find her luggage, imagining what her new life with her Aunty Ronke would be like. Lara had been told her aunt was a softer, kinder version of her mother. She imagined her to be like Mrs Oke, the glamorous mother of Temitope, one of her old schoolmates. Mrs

Oke always looked unmoved by the heat – as if there was an invisible air-conditioning cloud perched above her head accompanying her wherever she went. Her eyes were gracious and forgiving, her laugh, both girly and elegant, her smile magnified by the immaculate whiteness of her teeth... Every girl at her school secretly not-so-secretly wished Mrs Oke was their mother.

As passengers began to disperse, Lara looked around the arrivals lounge in awe and expectancy. Her heart was racing but it wasn't fear, it was the thrill of the new. Everything and everybody looked so bright, so shiny, so clean, so white... She had never seen so many white people. For her they only existed in films, in TV shows, in Enid Blyton books, where stories set in the countryside made her long for the green grass of England. And now, here she was. She breathed in deeply... Even the air felt different.

She heard her name called out by an unfamiliar voice. It came again. She turned to see a large fair-skinned Black woman with a speckled face in tight stonewashed jeans teamed with a wrinkled sweatshirt – the logo 'Armani' crooked on its front – that hugged the folds around her waist. Her short, curly wig, ill-fitting and frazzled, was the colour of Lucozade Original. Faux Birkenstocks smacked noisily beneath her feet.

The woman's smile was tight as she embraced her. 'Omolara,' she said, calling her by her full name. 'How was your flight?' Lara's body went stiff at the realization that the portly, unkempt woman in front of her was her aunt. Ronke took Lara's reaction as an affront. 'Ah what's wrong with you? You don't remember me?' she asked, twisting her face and cackling harshly. Her breath smelt stale. 'Why are you looking scared? *Oya* brings your suitcase.' She pointed at the carry-all. 'Is that one your bag, as well? Lara could only nod, the words in her head unable to make her way to her mouth. 'Okay,' Ronke said quickly. 'Let's go.'

The two of them headed to the exit as a slim-built, dark-skinned man with a skiffle, wide nose and a slight pot belly emerged from the crowd towards them. He reached for Lara's suitcase. 'Omolara! Look at you? You're a big girl now!' he said grinning. Knowing what was expected of her, Lara offered up a small, unsure smile. 'You were very small the last time we were in Nigeria,' he continued, 'Anyway, I'm your Uncle Wale,' he said, laughing, his chipped front tooth now visible, leaving Lara wondering where the joke was. She noticed 'Chelsea and Westminster Hospital' etched on the lanyard that hung from his neck. Her eyes wandered down the identification card to Wale's photo and name. Under it, Lara read the word 'Porter'.

'We have to go to church first,' Wale said apologetically. 'We are doing a special month of fasting. The children are already there. When we finish the service, we can go to the house. I hope you are not too tired?' He smiled at Lara kindly.

Not waiting for Lara to answer, Ronke interjected, 'Ah, if anybody should be complaining about sleep, it should be you, not Lara. She doesn't have to follow you to your night shift after church service. Lara will be okay.' She turned to her niece questioningly. '*Abi*?' Lara conceded politely with a nod. 'Anyway,' laughed Ronke, 'If you're tired, let's hope the spirit of the Lord will revive you, because you will need to look after the children during service and prepare their food when we get home.' Ronke pointed to a lavatory sign. 'Do you want the toilet before we go?'

Lara shook her head.

'Are you sure? The church is far, and we have to take public transportation. This country is not easy...' Ronke trailed off, then said, 'Anyway, are you one hundred percent sure you don't want to ease yourself? Open your mouth and talk,' she pressed impatiently.

'Yes, Aunty, I'm sure. Thank you, *Ma*,' Lara answered quietly.

'Okay. Let's go, let's go,' Ronke said, marching ahead to catch up with her husband.

From the corner of her eye, Lara could see the regal-looking navy-suited man who'd saved the day at Murtala Muhammad Airport. He was heading towards the car park, a man holding his luggage and suit carrier walking slightly ahead of him. If only, Lara thought, he could come and save the day now. Her heart began to race except it was no longer with excitement, it was fear. She suddenly yearned for the days of socializing with her friends as they devoured jollof rice and fried chicken neck at strangers funerals, for the gruffness of her grandmother's personality, for the bedlam of Mushin market, where the atmosphere lingered not with a foreign gloss, even-toned conversations and dependable air-conditioning but with untreated leather, old sweat and a heightened awareness of pickpockets… Lara suppressed the lump bubbling up at the back of her throat. She wanted to go home.

As she headed into the underground station with her aunt and uncle, beads of perspiration began to build on Lara's upper lip. She awkwardly carried her oversized piece of hand luggage on her shoulders, the crowd bustling and bumping past her in a way that felt unfamiliar. It was cold and aloof. The same air she'd breathed in with awe outside the arrivals sign now unnerved her.

'You're sweating?' noted Ronke with a laugh, looking ahead. 'Eh heh, I hope you are already seeing now what we are dealing with in this country. Everyone at home thinks life here is easy.' As the sound of the Piccadilly Line train began hurtling through the tunnel, Ronke turned to Lara with a strange smile that spoke of things to come. 'Welcome to London.'

HOUSE GIRL

'**N**KECHI!!'

Her head flew up. Quickly, she turned off the radio and kept perfectly still to really make sure she heard her name being called. The only thing that moved was the *thud, thud, thud* in her chest, caused by fear. And her overzealous dance moves and singing to Grady Harrell's 'Belinda'.

'NKECHI!!!'

Like the angry toot of Oga's car horn when Usman was too consumed in his marijuana-induced stupor to open the gate in time, it was unmistakable. Nkechi's head began to pound, matching her heartbeat. Her thoughts also became breathless with worry. So she didn't remember to answer. She moved towards the door in a panic and kicked over the large tray of black-eyed beans. '*Hei! Chineke*!!' Nkechi whispered the name of God in annoyance. She had spent the best part of two hours – in between dance routines – sifting through trays of beans, picking out stones and other foreign bodies that had the potential to make the evening dish – even when cooked in a seasoned stew of tomatoes, onions and peppers – totally inedible.

'NNNNN-KEEEE-CHIIIIIIII!!!'

It had only been a few seconds since she first heard her name being called but Madam Ogunnusi now sounded hoarse and hysterical, as if she had been hollering for her since the days of Elijah. In recent months, Madam's attitude towards her had become increasingly vitriolic.

'Yes, *Ma*! I'm coming, *Ma*! Sorry, *Ma*!' Nkechi replied, much too loudly. She was desperately trying to convey a calm and respectful tone coated with the expected sense of urgency. Inside, she rippled with apprehension. The beans would have to be cleared up afterwards. She hurriedly wiped her hands on the Ankara dress she wore; the bright blue and red bird print contrasted against the yellowness of her skin. Okoro, the man who sold palm wine back home in Uzuaba, used to say he wanted to spread her on his bread because her skin was the colour of Blue Band margarine. The thought of him eating *anything* with his black lips and kolanut-eroded teeth made Nkechi queasy. As she walked hurriedly while trying to adjust her rubber slippers, she slipped on the glossy tiled passage she had mopped just a few hours before. Steadying herself, she instinctively wiped her sweaty brow and palms on her dress again. Ever since a boy that lived in her grandmother's village had complained that holding her nervous hand was like handling dead catfish, wiping her hands had become habitual – even when her hands were bone dry. Nkechi took off her flip-flops and entered the parlour. Even now, she was still in awe of the soft, plush, thick pile carpet underfoot and the luxury of the air-conditioning. She had an old fan in her room. It was not particularly effective – it only worked if angled a certain way – but it was predictable and consistent. Here in the coolness of the parlour, depending on Madam's mood and whether Madam was in the room or not, Nkechi could easily be in heaven or hell. Today Madam was wearing a pink jacquard kaftan with a loosely fitted *gele* perched precariously on her head. Her outsized body, half laying, half sitting, balanced on the plump, cream leather sofa. Gold-hued mules were casually tossed by the edge of the mirrored side table. Her puffy unevenly pigmented face looked ghoulish as a result of the copious layers of Venus de Milo she wore like a mask. This cream, purchased in bulk on her trips to London, supposedly had the magical power to diminish the irate pimples on her heavily bleached face. Madam's eyes focused on *The Ten Commandments* on the huge television at the end of the capacious room – Charlton Heston had just parted the Red Sea – but Nkechi knew she was well aware of her presence. Even from the doorway, Nkechi could smell her renewed, heightened displeasure. It was pungent.

'I'm here, *Ma*. I'm very sorry, *Ma*; I didn't hear you before. I was in the kitchen doing the…' Nkechi's voice trailed off. She realized Madam was silent. She then curtsied apologetically, profusely, desperately. 'I'm very sorry, *Ma*,' she repeated. She noticed the empty beer bottles on the table.

Madam's eyes flared. Beads of perspiration decorated the white mask around her upper lip. She turned her girth towards her house girl. Her voice was mocking, menacingly so. 'What do you mean, "I was in the kitchen?!" In the kitchen DOING WHAT?! SINCE?!!! I have been calling you and calling you and CALLING YOU!!! So, if I was dying, I should have just died here because you were coming? Eh? I should have died because you and your deaf ears were coming?!'

'Mummy, I'm sorry…' Nkechi said, confused. She curtsied again, running her hot palms together, begging forgiveness.

Madam swiftly reached for one foot of her gold leather slippers and threw it in Nkechi's direction. Nkechi yelped and ducked. It missed, infuriating Madam all the more.

'WHO IS YOUR MUMMY? Who are you calling mummy?! Did I give birth to you? You, this village bastard. You better shut your dirty mouth. Did I tell you to talk?! *E no go better for you.*' She stretched her fingers out in a star shape and began to curse her, '*Oloshi Olori Buruku.* Idiot.'

She breathed heavily and took a swig from a bottle of Guilder as if rewarding herself for a hard day's work. She burped loudly, closing her eyes for a few seconds before turning to Nkechi again 'Why are you just standing there? Bring back my slipper!'

'Yes, *Ma*!' Nkechi quickly went to pick up the weapon that almost took out her eye. She braced herself as she walked closer to Madam and placed the slipper with its twin, ensuring the 'Made in Italy' labels were aligned. She took a deep breath, expecting the heat of Madam's fat hands across the back of her neck. Nothing. She stood up waiting for her orders. Madam's eyes had already gone back to the screen. The waters were closing in on the Egyptian army. Nkechi stood still for what felt like a week. Madam eventually looked round at her – as if she were a mosquito, still alive, still being a nuisance.

'You're still here?!! You want me to get up and slap your yellow face? You don't have things to do? What do you want?'

Nkechi was awkward. 'Erm, Madam, sorry, you called me... I came because you called me.'

If Madam was embarrassed at her gaffe, her face hid it well. 'Get the remote from that table and stop the video. Change it to NTA – I want to see the news.'

Nkechi picked up the controls and pressed the buttons accordingly. Of course, Madam could have reached easily if only she stretched her bulk, but she never moved unless she really had to, hence her size.

'Leave it here,' Madam said motioning towards the side table closest to her head. As Nkechi bent forward, at last, she felt Madam's fist plummet into her cheek. The force of which – along with a simultaneous kick – left Nkechi on the floor. No altercation was complete without it. 'Next time, if I have to call you more than ONCE, that's the day you will go home to those useless gods they serve in that your backward village! If you are hard of hearing, go and clean your rotten ears. GET OUT. Make sure those beans are ready before everybody gets here.'

'Yes, *Ma*.' Nkechi held her face as she sprinted out of the room. She put the radio back on in the kitchen, lowering the volume. The last thirty seconds of 'Islands in the Stream' played before the DJ threw in 'She's a Bad Mama Jama'. This time she didn't sing along for fear of not hearing the next time she was summoned. Besides, her face hurt too much. With one hand holding a cup of ice water to her cheek, Nkechi bent down and began to pick up the beans one by one.

The beans were half cooked by the time Nkechi heard the requisite hoot of the car at the main gate. Usman had probably fallen asleep again. Last week, Oga lost his temper with him. 'Usman, what is wrong with you? Do you have sleeping sickness? Why do we have you here? Will you snore like a swine until armed robbers come and carry the house away?' Oga asked, his voice low but brimming with irritation. If Madam was delivering the reprimand, of course, it would have come with an all-inclusive slap. But Oga was much more laid-back, as Nkechi had come to understand. The kitchen was unbearably hot – she was looking forward to the moment she could walk through the air-conditioned visitor's passage that led to the front of the house. She stirred raw corn into the pot, washed her hands and hurried to the main entrance. Being at the door to meet, greet and carry bags for Oga, the family and their frequent visitors was something expected of her. This and other duties – spoken and unspoken – were things that never left her unwritten checklist. Waking at 4:30A.M. to prepare hot baths and breakfast for the household. Tick. Washing and ironing every day. Tick. Taking their youngest daughter Tinuke to have her hair braided in intricate styles like patewo. Tick. Never conversing with visitors unless they spoke to her first. Tick. Grinding pepper weekly at the market. Tick. Cooking. Tick. Providing regular sex to the Oga of the house. Tick. Whenever he wanted it. Tick. However, he wanted it. Tick. Tick. Tick.

The first time Oga turned up at her room, she thought he was sleepwalking. She had heard that it is possible for people to do this. It was an unusually cool night. She did not feel her *wrapper* being lifted from her. Until the breeze hit her flesh. From the time they were old enough to understand, her mother drummed into her and her siblings that regardless of how hot or cool the nights were, they were never to go to bed naked 'because if the house is burning down, you will forget yourself and run out for the whole neighbourhood to see. If everyone has seen your *yansh*, who will marry you?' The Ogunnusi's house, unlike her childhood home, was made with concrete and the finest materials. Nkechi doubted houses like these ever burned down. As she sluggishly tried pulling back the cloth over her shoulders, her hand met with another. The hand was big and chubby – soft, spoilt, rich-people palms. She was suddenly wide awake and, with the aid of the moonlight that streamed through her louver window, saw Oga before her in his St Michael's vest and pant. She knew it was from the London store because she was the one who washed it. linking to attention, she sat up slightly and asked, in her naivete, if he needed anything, if he needed her to make him food or to get him a drink. He stooped down and began to position half of his weight on her large, uncovered mattress. The other half was on her. He was heavy. 'It's not food that is doing me right now. You are not a small girl anymore. You know what I want.' His voice was playful. She smelt something sharp on his breath. Could he be *that* drunk? she wondered. She was desperate to cover herself, but he held on to her while his other hand started to pull down the only thing she had on.

'Please, Oga,' she whispered fearfully. 'Please Oga, I no want this kind thing. Please. I no want Madam's trouble. Please.' He just laughed thickly. 'Nkechi, I've been watching you. Your body is sweet. Sweet body.' Oga's breath across her chest was hot. She felt his hand between her legs. She would have listened to her mother and worn clothes to bed. The truth was it never protected her in the past. A strange fright had crippled her so she knew screaming would emit no sound. Perhaps it was to do with the authority at which he had removed her underwear. Perhaps because this was Oga, and who would have the audacity to scream at Oga? Perhaps because as the minutes went by, there was that voice, the one that lived in her dark cloud that told her she should keep quiet and be grateful. She should feel privileged. Privileged that Oga, the most powerful barrister in the town should want *her*, Nkechi, a barely educated fifteen-year-old village girl. The voice also told her it was her fault it kept happening. It was her fault that by the age of ten she already had a woman's body. She whispered frantically, 'Oga, please, I no want this. Oga, I beg you, stop.'

He stopped talking, breathing hard instead. When he finally spoke, his voice was hoarse and unrecognizable as he commanded, 'Open your leg! You're not a small girl. This is not the body of a small girl... I'm sure this can't be your first time...Yes, yes... Open it.' She stopped fighting. When it ended, he readjusted his underwear and with a yawn and a stretch, he left.

That was just over three years ago. It marked the return of the dark clouds that threatened to crush her for as long as she could remember. Before her father died, the dark clouds rarely left her. The villagers all whispered, about her and her 'madness' – the strength of which was so melancholic, no wealth of local, herbal concoctions could quench. Once he was dead, she hoped her dark clouds would die with him.

Here in Lagos, their visits were not as often and not as long, so they were easier to hide. The group of local, house girls she came to befriend assumed she was just homesick. The rest of the house help – the gateman, the driver – excused it as the result of a young girl at the sharp end of Madam's perennial wrath. Nobody else noticed. Least of all Oga. Not even on the occasions she simply closed her eyes and lay inert like a block of cement until it was over. Whenever the dark clouds lifted – sometimes they left as abruptly as they arrived – she vowed that she would find a supernatural boldness, to refuse him, to fight him, to confront him like she should have done with her own father all those years ago. But she didn't. Because how does one speak the unspeakable? Speaking the unspeakable was to acknowledge the acts her own father forced upon her after hours, acts her mother pretended to be blind and deaf to. And so Nkechi did the same and stayed silent in her dark cloud. After he died, she was finally able to leave for Lagos. If it was her choice she would have left like many girls her age, at least three years earlier. Agents, including her uncle, approached her father, making him aware of the financial benefits that come with sending your daughter to become a maid in the capital. He refused. The day after he was buried, Nkechi left.

She'd recently begun attending Sunday service with one of the born-again house girls that lived nearby. Nkechi hadn't been to church since leaving home. She still remembered her father preaching from the pulpit that church was where one went to be cleansed, to be redeemed, to be strengthened. And yet. She still couldn't find the strength to tell Oga, no. Also, he always caught her off-guard. She never saw clues during the day. He just turned up when he turned up. His sons being home and visits from his mother-in-law were not deterrents. Sometimes there were long absences. He never explained. And she never asked him to. She wouldn't dare. She wasn't foolish enough to think she was the only one. She too had heard the rumours. And as much as she created scenarios in her head, she knew their 'relationship' was not the love affairs she read about in the faded tattered Mills & Boons her friend Aina lent her. Oga never attempted to kiss her. One night she forgot herself and went against his implicit no intimacy rule. She imagined they were actual lovers, that this was her choice, and she began to caress his neck. It was quickly met with a rebuff leaving her deeply embarrassed, a shameful reminder of what was real.

He also discouraged conversation. One night she whispered, 'I haven't seen my menses.' When he didn't respond, she mistook his silence for a lack of comprehension and so for emphasis added, 'I'm late. I've waited... No blood is coming' hoping this would cut into his muteness. That night, he left without touching her. Under her door the next morning was a bulky envelope. A rough piece of paper was placed in front of the thick wad of money. Someone had scrawled a Surulere address on it. This was where she had the first of her two abortions.

Nkechi headed to the car. The big status-symbol car imported from *'ovasees'*. The sun was still beating hard causing her blouse to stick to her back.

'Welcome, *Sa*,' she curtsied as she greeted Oga and his teen sons back home from their boarding school. Her hand shook slightly as she grabbed their hand luggage and led the way into the house. Usman, and Ibrahim – the driver – carried the heavier pieces and followed behind her. She spoke to them while looking ahead, disdainfully reminding them to 'leave those your *yama yama* shoes outside.' She twisted her face as she imagined Usman's ashy mangled hoofs and the sixth toe that grew on the side of Ibrahim's right foot. She made a mental note that next time they went through the house, they must both go through the side entrance. She had spent hours the day before cleaning all the floors. The last thing she needed was her workload increasing. As they dropped pieces of luggage outside the relevant bedrooms, Ibrahim sung softly to himself. Nkechi's smile was wry. Everywhere she went she heard, '*Belinda eh eh, Belinda oh oh Belinda.*' It was '*Belinda eh eh*' that got her into trouble earlier that day. Usman, the more sombre of the two, was quiet. They finally reached the end of the hallway by the master bedroom and dropped the final case. It was the eighth and biggest bedroom in the house. It also housed two dressing rooms, a sitting area and a bathroom. It was bigger than the entire house Nkechi had shared with her four siblings and parents.

'Okay, you people can go now.' Nkechi needn't have said anything. Usman and Ibrahim knew they were not to set foot in that room. Usman turned on his heel to go through the entrance they came. 'No, no, go this way.' Nkechi signalled towards the back entrance. He stared at her before turning and walking away. He didn't utter a word, but his *ganga*-infused eyes said it all: *Don't fool yourself. You will never be one of them.* Nkechi was embarrassed, flustered, and hated herself for it. He was just the gateman. Why should his opinion bother her? Perhaps she was just imagining his judgmental, jaundiced eyes.

'So, Nkechi, how now? Every day, you *de* look more and more fine for body, *o! Kai*!' Ibrahim's teasing voice jostled her thoughts. He posed with one hand in his pocket, eyeing her from head to toe. Her friend, Aina, always marvelled at Ibrahim's confidence. Even with his pervasive sweat patches, big face, unusual tribal marks and those splayed *katafuru* buck teeth, he still conversed with women like he was a god.

Nkechi rolled her eyes. '*Abeg*, Ibrahim, go trouble your wife or you don forget say you have one at home?'

He laughed, 'Why you de talk like that? You know *na* you be my *tru tru* wife.' He was about to lean in closer when his name echoed down the corridor. He jumped to attention and scurried towards Oga's oncoming voice, telling him to re-park the car at the other end of the compound as Oga would not be going out again that day.

Nkechi had already started to move the case into the bedroom when Oga came in. He sat on the bed – his weight causing a deep dent, creasing the fresh cotton sheets – and looked intently at the paperwork in his hands. She was taking his suit carrier and weekend case to the dressing room when he looked up at her. 'Just leave it there,' he said irritably, which meant that he wanted her to leave.

'Yes, *Sa*,' she replied quietly. She needed no further instruction and walked hurriedly out of the room. She always thought it amazing how, like so many of the rich people that formed their circle of friends, he was wholeheartedly able to look through people like her. His eyes barely displayed recognition, much less sentiment. And yet that same night, she was to him like water to a man dying of thirst.

The next day, Nkechi began to set the table in the grand dining room for a small dinner party. Dr Ajala and the much younger Mrs Ajala (the second) were coming that evening. They would be bringing his overweight and unusually self-assured teenage daughters from his first marriage. As she put out the gold-trimmed cutlery the way she had been taught, the family prepared for the arrival of their guests. She could hear the powerful rush of the shower behind one of the bedroom doors. From another room, she heard, as she did on countless occasions, Madam and Oga arguing. As usual, it was mostly Madam's threatening voice. Nkechi was surprised when Oga's menace matched his wife's. 'You are talking NONSENSE! Shut your mouth RIGHT NOW!' Nothing else was in English. In her three years with the family, Nkechi still struggled to speak or understand Yoruba fluently. She understood enough to greet. She understood enough to haggle. She understood enough to curse – it was, after all, the language Madam used on her. The shower stopped. She made a mental note to pick up the dirty laundry later. She kept an ear out for Madam's sluggish moneyed footsteps. It's what she called 'Rich People Walking'. When the house girls met at the market, conversation would inevitably turn to the latest gist on the wealthy families they all worked for. Aina, the clown and matriarch of the group, loved mimicking the *laisse faire* saunter of Mrs Ajala the second, the madam of her household. 'Why should they rush around sweating like pigs when they have people like us to do it for them?' The injustices of being treated as if they had leprosy was also always topical. One of the girls once told of her employer's seven-year-old son refusing to eat for fear she may have 'touched and breathed on' his plate because her hands and lips were 'too black'. She was instructed by her light-skinned Madam to wear white gloves and a scarf around her mouth while serving his food. They all gasped. Nkechi thought how much wider their mouths and eyes would open at the things Oga instructed her to do.

Madam was checking over her dishes – *asaro*, jollof rice, *ewedu* for the pounded yam, assorted meat stew. Nkechi stood to attention as she was given firm orders as to how to serve when the guests arrive. 'Make sure you use those white and gold China plates,' Madam reminded her curtly. 'Bring out those big glasses Oga brought from his last trip to London. Put the rest of the minerals in the freezer. They need to be very cold. Make sure you take them out in time. They must not break. If they break, I will break you.'

Just before everyone arrived, Nkechi put Tinuke to bed. She then quickly splashed water on her face, dusted powder on her armpits and changed her dress. (Halfway through giving her instructions, Madam suddenly said, 'If you think you're going to serve us food wearing that stinking thing, you're mad.') As the guests exchanged pleasantries with their hosts, Nkechi brought out the freezing cold soft drinks. She timed it so the bottles, thankfully, did not break. Shortly afterwards, the family and guests took their seats in the dining room and Nkechi began to serve as she had been instructed earlier. Dr Ajala, loud, gregarious, always chuckling at his own jokes, debated local government corruption with Oga. The fat twins – as Ngozi and their maid, Aina, secretly referred to them – were vying for the attention of Kayode, the Ogunnusis' eldest son. He teased and flirted with his newly low voice and chiselled features, knowing the plump duo didn't stand a chance in hell. Nkechi had noted his type; all the girls that he brought home were girls for whom food wasn't a major priority. Madam was in high spirits, as was the coquettish Mrs Ajala, although hers was not alcohol induced. Nkechi once overheard Madam on the phone gossiping about her guest, referring to her as a 'husband stealer'. Mrs Ajala the second had remained Dr Ajala's mistress even while the original wife wasted away from a rare blood disorder. Though seemingly imperceptible to the men, it was clear Madam and the new Mrs Ajala were not members of the mutual appreciation club. There was a look of pure loathing on Madam's face when Mrs Ajala refused second helpings and laughingly announced, tapping her flat stomach, 'I am watching my weight.'

Nkechi took extra drinks and snacks into the parlour where the guests moved to and stayed for the remainder of the evening. She cleared the dining room and called Usman and Ibrahim to join her in eating what was left. They made their way into the utility area, which housed a couple of broken, discarded chairs, Nkechi's radio which she'd inherited from her predecessor: a huge plastic drum filled with ice and a metal pail that Ibrahim usually turned upside down to sit on.

'So,' started Ibrahim, chuckling as he gnawed noisily on a fried chicken foot, 'what is happening in the parlor? Is Madam already drunk and disgracing her poor husband again?' He laughed louder as Usman shook his head. Ibrahim put down the bone and bit into a piece of tripe. 'You people are acting like I am blaspheming. Isn't it the truth I'm telling?'

Nkechi replied, 'Abeg, finish what is in your mouth before talking to us. She has been okay this evening. If not for her, would we be sitting here eating this food?'

Ibrahim, his left cheek bulging, looked up, incredulous. 'Ah, are you okay? Since when did you become her best friend? So, because you went to church last week, you are now Mary, mother of Christ? And so what that she has given us food tonight? Should we starve? I feel sorry for Oga. Who can blame him for having girlfriends all over Lagos. A wife should respect her husband. If the mother of my children was always misbehaving, shaming me in front of people...' He shook his head and carried on chewing on his tripe.

Nkechi bristled – was it guilt? Or shame? 'Ibrahim, what are you talking about? So a man should be carrying women up and down and the wife should be happy about it? Can you blame her for drinking?'

Ibrahim took a gulp of water and replied, 'Nkechi, there are more men than women in this world. I'm sure you know that. It is a man's right to have as many women as he wants. You better find your peace with that. If you don't, you will never get married.'

Although she was well used to overlooking Ibrahim's customary chauvinistic remarks, tonight it riled her. 'I feel sorry for your wife and children,' she responded, her anger bubbling.

Ibrahim laughed heartily. 'Ah, Nkechi, no vex, I go take you out and teach you everything *wey* you need know. I can prepare you.' Even hard-faced Usman could not resist a sly chuckle.

She got up as she kissed her teeth at Ibrahim and said, 'You're very foolish.' To which he responded with a louder hoot fully bearing the wide gap between his two front teeth.

'Nkechi!' For once, Nkechi was glad to hear the sound of Madam bellowing her name throughout the house. She had already lost her appetite; the rice had begun to taste like sand in her mouth.

That night, Nkechi couldn't sleep. The heat didn't help, and she couldn't get Ibrahim's comments out of her head, where her dark cloud now began to form. Nkechi decided yet again that she would tell Oga she could no longer carry on. His visits had been less frequent in recent months, anyway. Imagining her telling him NO gave her crippling nausea. Surely he wouldn't violently force her (Was the first time violent? There was force but at least he didn't beat her. Not like her father. Is this different? Better?) Surely, he has more than enough women? He didn't *need* her. But then again for rich Nigerians, was it ever about need? They didn't need the four expensive cars in the driveway and yet there they were.

A few days later Oga came into her room. And perhaps this time her dark cloud suddenly gave her supernatural powers and just like that she found the boldness and told him, 'Oga, I no want this again. I no like this. Please. I no want again,' hoping he couldn't hear the shake in her voice. His face was expressionless as he opened the door again and gently closed it behind him. She was left pondering over the brevity of their exchange for well over an hour, after which she fell into the deepest sleep she'd had for as long as she could remember, her dark cloud lifting.

Over the next week she went about her duties with a newfound lightness. Still, she had moments of flashbacks, moments of regret, moments of longing. Longing for who she could have been, the girl who loved to dream, the girl she was before she was soiled. There was another sense of longing that made her hot with shame. Not a longing for Oga. No, not for someone else's husband. But maybe a husband of her own. Maybe. She didn't know how; with her father now dead, who would pay her dowry? Her disabled mother and younger siblings lived off whatever meagre wages she earned. She had no idea how much it was; she saw none of it, the understanding was that every kobo would go straight home. That she had food to eat and a roof over her head was enough. But it wasn't enough. This, she scolded herself, is the problem with reading too many Mills & Boons. Yes, you have improved your English, but you have also allowed yourself to believe in dreams. Her father once told her that girls who are no longer pure could not afford to dream. She had just begun drifting into sleep, when she heard the familiar creek of the door. Nkechi kept her eyes closed, her heart racing. Why is he here? Did her no not mean no? She felt his hand – it felt oddly rough and clammy... She opened her eyes and she cried out in horror, 'Usman!' Nkechi could smell he was high. 'Usman,' she repeated, 'what are you doing here? Please leave this place! I take God name beg you, don't touch me, just leave this place!' Nkechi barely recognized her frightened voice.

Usman laughed cruelly. 'Which God you *dey* call? Now you know God? You no know God when you *dey* open your legs for Oga? You no know God when you treat me like cockroach just because you *dey* sex with Oga?' Her leg kicked the empty soft-drinks bottles stored in the crates at the end of her bedside. It made a crashing sound. The nightlight shone on Usman's panicked face. Beads of sweat peppered his forehead, and his eyes were red. He stood suddenly and held his head in his hands as Nkechi pulled the sheet around herself. He quickly left the room leaving Nkechi untouched but trembling on her sweaty mattress.

Over the next few weeks, the dark cloud returned and stayed. Nkechi did everything she could to avoid Usman. He in turn did the same. When they did collide, she didn't meet his eye. Her stance was brisk and businesslike. He, on the other hand, seemed contrite. She knew she had to forgive; otherwise how else would God forgive her? But the cloud wouldn't let go and for now she could not let go of how Usman had shamed her. Ibrahim was, as usual, jolly, unaffected, whistling away. He was at a loose end, as Oga had him on standby for a drive into town later. He busied himself filling Nkechi in on his latest conspiracy theory. Normally, at the very least, she would find it entertaining. Recent events had left her uptight, sensitive and nauseous. So today, she wasn't in the mood.

'Didn't I say it?' she could hear Ibrahim say. 'Didn't I say you should watch and see? These types of women are never satisfied. I mean, what will a woman like that be looking for in an ugly man like Dr Ajala if not for his money?' He paused while he snapped open a bottle of Sprite with his teeth. He didn't wait for Nkechi's reply, she was focused on hanging up the washing, and he instead answered his own question. 'Of course it is money.' He quickly followed his loud burp with a 'Sorry', to which Nkechi responded with a look of repulsion. Nevertheless, he carried on speaking. 'But who can blame her? Now she is the official wife and has the money, she wants a better-looking man... Oga is big but still fine for face. I've seen the way she laugh with Oga when her husband is not around... And Oga, too, laughing with her, opening ALL his teeth...'

Nkechi, throwing her basket of pegs down as they walked back to the house, said, 'Ibrahim, don't you have anything to do than use your mouth to spread rumours about the people that are paying your salary?' Ibrahim looked bruised as he walked away. She wanted to call him back to apologize, but then heard Madam calling her name from the sitting room. To Nkechi's ears, Madam sounded calm and – dare she think it – pleasant. Something was wrong.

'Yes, *Ma*, I'm coming,' she replied quickly and made haste down the corridor as she wiped her hand on the same Ankara she was wearing on the day Madam threw the gold slipper at her.

As she entered the sitting room Nkechi said, 'I'm here, Mada—' She was stunned to see her uncle in the room, sitting on a single chair while Madam and Oga sat opposite him on the sofa. She ran to him. 'Uncle! What are you doing here? Is everything okay? Has somebody died?' He was the one who brought her here four years ago. Everyone in the village knew he could help to place their young daughters with middle-class Lagosian families. For her mother, whose legs were severely injured following a farming accident, it was a lifeline. Nkechi momentarily forgot herself and started speaking in Igbo until her uncle rose and slapped her face so hard she felt as if her cheek had been hit by a lorry. She staggered back in bewilderment. His broken English was heavy with anger and gesticulation. 'Nkechi, you come disgrace *una* family for this place? *Eh*? *Na* that we send you for *Akwu-na-kwuna*? *Eh*? he asked heatedly as he accused her of prostitution. Nkechi burst into tears and fell to her knees in front of him. He pushed her away with a force that almost toppled her.

Oga stood up to interrupt. 'Please, let us do this without too much strife. Please,' his hand gestured to the older man, 'take your seat.' He sat back down, joining his wife on the couch. 'Nkechi, get up and sit down in that chair. Anyway, this won't take long.'

Madam said nothing. She had a strange look on her face.

Once Nkechi was seated, Oga looked in her direction, his eyes lacking emotion and began to speak as she could imagine he did when giving a summation at court. 'I'm sure

Nkechi, you are wondering why we are here today.' At that point, Madam sighed dramatically and folded her arms across her heaving bosom. Oga ignored her and continued. 'I'm not going to waste time talking too much. You and Usman. So how long were you going to continue sleeping with him under this roof?'

Nkechi was so shocked she almost gagged. 'Usman? Me and Usman?! I didn't do anything with Usman!' she cried out as she fell to her knees once again, pleading her innocence.

This time it was Madam who rose to her feet to interrupt. 'Shut up and stop denying!' she shouted. 'You still have the effrontery to defend yourself after we saw Usman coming out of your room with our own eyes.'

'No, no, no!' By now Nkechi was choking on her sobs. She turned to her relative who sat stony-faced. 'Uncle please believe me; I didn't do anything... He came to the room. I told him to leave me. I didn't I didn't...' She couldn't stop crying.

Oga spoke kindly to Nkechi's uncle. 'You see, like I was saying before, Usman has been with us for many years. He is a very quiet man and from what I have understood, Nkechi has been flirting with him and this is what it has now come to. This man is a devout Muslim, and we have forgiven him because we know this is not the kind of thing he would do ordinarily. It is not his fault – Nkechi has been trying to tempt him for a long time and he had a moment of weakness. You see, many of these young girls, it is what they do these days. Then when they are exposed, they will say the man raped them. As innocent as she seems, Nkechi has been uselessing herself. We saw with our own eyes.'

Nkechi flung her hands over her head and screamed '*Chineke!* Usman *don* finish me! *Na lie*!! *Na lie*!!' To which Madam shouted, 'Shut up! You are the only liar here – and you still have mouth to talk!'

Oga calmly continued. 'We need to have people here we can trust to behave themselves. Who knows just how many other boys around town she has been messing around with? A young woman should not be behaving like this. And definitely not in this God-fearing home.' He now looked directly at his house girl, ignoring her desperate, searching eyes. 'You should go and pack your bags,' he said without emotion.

At this point, her uncle also started to plead with his niece's employers. 'Please, I beg you, please *una* have mercy, you know *na* her salary *dey* feed the family back home. You know she no get father. Please, Oga, Sir...' He rubbed his palms together, his lined face pitiful as he also begged Madam. 'Please, *Ma*, please, I beg, oh, have mercy...please...'

Madam moved back from him as if he were contaminated, shaking her head 'This is not a begging matter. We have a small daughter; we have to protect her from bad examples. We cannot stand for this. Nkechi has been pretending she is innocent. She needs to pack her bags. She has to go today.

She has to go NOW. We have already found someone to take her place.'

Nkechi's uncle cried out spectacularly and began to prostrate before Madam, at which point Nkechi stopped crying. A wash of indignation engulfed her as she saw her bereft uncle, dressed in his old, faded Ankara with his dusty feet so out of place on the expensive carpet, begging these people that looked at him, at them, with such disdain. She grabbed him before he reached the floor. 'Uncle, please... please,' she said. Please, Uncle....' Her tone was now firm. She helped to raise the slight, defeated man to his feet before evenly announcing to him in Igbo that she was going to collect her things and meet him outside. She went to her room and began throwing the little she had into a 'Ghana Must Go' bag. She began to feel faint and was now just desperate to get out of the house. She turned and was startled by Madam standing in the doorway.

'Madam, please, I am just taking my things. You can even check my bag,' she said opening the bag as she walked towards her. 'I did not steal anything.'

Madam looked straight at her and laughed bitterly. '*Eh heh*, you mean like you tried to steal my husband?' Nkechi's mouth opened and closed again. No sound came out.

'Oh, you think I didn't know?' said Madam. 'You think drinking Guilder makes me blind and deaf? You think I'm a fool? My husband can go outside and sleep with whoever he wants but you think you, you this small rat of a house girl can continue sleeping with my husband under MY own roof?'

Nkechi began to cry again, whispering, 'Please forgive me. I didn't ask him to come to my room. I wasn't trying to steal him Madam. I didn't want—'

Madam spat directly in Nkechi's face. 'Don't insult me,' she hissed angrily. 'You have insulted me enough. Let me tell you, if you don't know, it was me that sent Usman to go to your room and made sure my husband saw him coming out. Next time, you decide to spread your legs for another woman's husband, you will remember that not all women are as stupid as you.' Madam walked away and Nkechi cleaned off the tears and the thick mucus that had begun sliding out of her nose. She took the back entrance of the house to where her uncle was waiting with Ibrahim. His hand was raised above his brow as protection against the sun which shone bright and fierce.

'Oga said I should drop you somewhere you can take transport.' Ibrahim sounded official but Nkechi knew him long enough to trace the sadness in his voice. Going through the main gate, they passed Usman going about his daily duties. He turned his back on the car.

They rode along in complete silence until it became unbearable for Ibrahim, and he turned on the radio. '*Belinda, eh eh, Belinda, oh oh, Belinda…*' This time Nkechi didn't dance, and Ibrahim didn't hum. He kept his eyes firmly on the road. It was only when they arrived at the bus stop and her now stony-faced uncle stepped out of the car that Ibrahim turned to her, his usual jovial features now in cheerless mode. He mouthed 'Sorry.' Too numb to respond, Nkechi simply nodded.

As she watched him speed away, bag over her shoulder, the earlier queasiness in her body returned. Being a house girl was her ticket out of Uzuaba. Unlike some of the girls who had gone before her, she was eager to go to Lagos. After her father died, her mother said Nkechi's face was too painful to look at. The village life awaiting Nkechi was the life her mother had had: working on the farm, digging yams, looking after her siblings, fetching water from the stream, all while waiting for an arranged marriage to a useless man who would see nothing wrong in beating her to a pulp because the stew didn't have enough salt in it, and sleeping with their eldest daughter. Lagos presented a form of escape. And hope for a new life. Nkechi's queasiness increased. Then suddenly, with a terrifying clarity, her nausea felt…familiar. It was the same…but different. This time there was no money-stuffed envelope accompanied by a handwritten address in Surulere where the seed of her nausea miraculously disappears. The realization made Nkechi feel faint. She boarded the over-crowded *molue* bus with her uncle and when they began speeding along the expressway, she heard the screams of the fellow passengers as she threw herself out through the doors.

THE TAIL OF A SMALL LIZARD

In the run-up to leaving Nigeria, I considered dropping you a written confession. I planned to leave it with your gateman. (Your gateman who was always praying – too loud, always too loud – on his special Mecca mat. Like so many of us Muslims – except perhaps failed ones like me – he seemed convinced that a certain, consistent level of fervency guaranteed his place in heaven.) I imagined I'd seal the letter Fort Knox-style, but seeing as the only thing he read was the *Quran*, I realized it wouldn't matter. And then I talked myself out of it. Because none of what happened was actually my fault. I was not there; I was not the perpetrator. This is what I told myself. And on a good day, it worked. But most days were not good days.

My therapist says it's time to face my demons. Oh yes, I have a therapist. I know. It's so very un-Nigerian. But every-one in New York has a therapist. When I started getting bigger modelling contracts that moved me from London to Paris (my French is still horrible) and then finally to New York a few years back, my agent negotiated deals that came with all kinds of ridiculous perks – cleaners, trainers, weekly massages, a chef, a therapist... I remember being told it's the city that never sleeps, and so you will be expected not to sleep. Of course they were jesting with the truth. When you work in fashion, you spend more time awake than most normal people. The hours are long, the parties relentless, and the pressure to stay at the top of the game is intense. But that's not the reason I've stopped sleeping.

I have disturbing dreams. They are, of course, nightmares. I keep seeing the face of Mr Olumide, the bus driver back home. He was always having accidents. Small ones, initially. But nevertheless, accidents. Which is ironic, considering his great-grandfather was the one who started the God Is Behind Your Wheel bus company.

When Mr Olummide's yellow bus crashed that day, I don't think any God was behind that wheel. Just a terrible driver with unchecked cataracts. A driver who, along with most of the passengers, perished. In my dreams, I keep seeing women's unravelled *bubas* in lace and *Ankara*, their crushed matching *geles* and the produce they bought from

Onitsha market. Seeds peeking out of ruptured overripe mangoes, the eye-watering scent from flattened red and yellow *ata rodo*, rancid dried fish – I can smell it, even now. There was also a dirty cow foot – just one. A split sack of *garri* decorating the road like sand. Three catfish, still alive, dancing, dancing, dancing, till their breath suddenly stops. Like the food, bodies are also scattered everywhere. So many dead bodies.

Months later, preposterous tales about the crash continued to fuel the horrors in my head. They said half of Mr Gori's brain was spilling out of his head and rested on his left shoulder. (I would never have imagined that the local welder had such a big brain. If he did, it was no indication of his level of intelligence.) Then there were stories about the blood from the passengers, which had begun to darken as it mixed with drippings from a crushed carton of meat – a sacrificial lamb, of sorts – murdered early that morning. I imagined so much blood that it ran like a stream. Like in Exodus, when God put the plague on Egypt. (My therapist once remarked that considering I have issues with a belief system, my analogies are strangely, innately, religious. I told her these were the joys of growing up in Nigeria.)

Mama Kemi, my grandmother, Alhaja's, childhood friend, was one of the passengers on that bus that day. Her presence was totally by happenstance; it was not her usual market day. She decided to go earlier in the week to fill the oversized Zanussi refrigerator given to her by her daughter from the US – 'you know the one, the one married to the big lawyer' – she'd always boast. She needed to completely fill it because, she believed, 'an empty fridge will bring a life marinated with emptiness'. We Yorubas always concoct ridiculous superstitions to justify irrational behaviour. The reality was less convoluted: her much-hated in-laws were visiting, and she wanted them to burn with envy.

She was one of the five who survived the bus crash, but the shock left her bedbound. And so, for twenty-one days, her family and fellow white-garmented congregants from the Cherubim and Seraphim Church prayed. For twenty-one days, they bathed her with holy water and oiled her body with the holy oil. For twenty-one days, her family abstained from food. Even her visiting distant, second cousin, Ms Deola, a reluctant spinster who wasn't part of the church or even a believer, joined in the fast, seeing it as an opportunity to shed her girth. Despite the prayers and rituals, nothing worked; Mama Kemi remained alive but lifeless. There were times I'd visit her and she would cry these strange silent tears, staring at me as she did so. Staring as if she knew my hand in everything. It was frightening.

A few months after the accident, the town seemed to have gradually gone back to normal, on the surface: the cocks resumed their crowing; the shops reopened; children went to school; the fleet of churchgoers from various denominations went by on Sunday mornings; the warm comforting smell from the bakery began, once again, permeating the air at 5:00A.M. Laughter was, once again, heard on the street. And yet an unease lingered.

Most unnerving for me was when Alhaja stopped eating. Where my mother was flighty, my grandmother operated like clockwork. And that included her appetite; she was a large woman who famously – unless it was Ramadan – enjoyed and celebrated the ritual of food. But not now. Not while the undercurrent of community grief remained. Still, she encouraged me to eat: 'We need meat on these your small, small bones,' she'd say, the shiny gold tooth she acquired on her pilgrimage to Mecca sparkling in her mouth. Her smile didn't reach her eyes or her heart. But at the time I would eat to keep her quiet. And then afterwards. I would go by the *shalanga* at the very far back of the house and put my fingers down my throat to purge myself. It was only when I moved to London that I heard the word 'bulimia'. And it was always connected to weight loss. If that's the case, then I am an incompetent bulimic, because my weight has more or less remained the same. My therapist tells me it was never – and still is not – about weight. When you have an unmarried, sexually free but detached mother who gave birth to you (reluctantly) in her teens, a father you never met, and a part in a bus crash that killed fifty-three people, you, too, might spend your life trying to throw up shame.

I first met Bakare when he came to live with his grandmother, Iya Eleni – she owned the shop selling mats next door to my grandmother's grocery store. He had recently returned from London after only seven months, because, he explained, 'The cold didn't agree with me.' Everyone knew he had been deported.

We had very little in common. Or so I initially thought. I was thirteen; he was nineteen. I was a voracious reader; he had barely completed his first year of secondary school. I could smell trouble on him – and not the attractive kind – and he initially dismissed me, saying I acted like a born-again Christian girl (a comment that, particularly for a Muslim, was meant to be deeply insulting; but his English was so threadbare, nothing he said could make me feel inferior to him). And yet, slowly we came to realize, without really articulating it, that there was a connection between us. We both had mother issues. (His considered him too difficult, which is why he lived with his grandmother. Mine was too caught up with her transactional romances to pay any attention to me, and so I was essentially brought up by my grandmother, too.) We also had absent fathers. (Bakare never met his. I knew mine, but did I? For as long as I could remember, he was always drunk, and his appearances were few and far between. I couldn't truly profess to know him.)

Bakare and I were both dissatisfied with where we were in our lives – physically and otherwise – and craved a way out. My planned route was education – I didn't want to be like my mother; her passport through life was via the pockets of very wealthy, ultimately unavailable, men. Bakare's flight path to achieving his freedom? I didn't dare ask but I imagined it would be through any means necessary. There was an undercurrent of anger that lived in Bakare. Everything and everyone apart from me and his grandmother seemed to irritate him. Life itself riled him. Nevertheless, we bonded. I was tall for my age, a lanky, socially awkward late bloomer, dressed in oversized sports T-shirts and shapeless shorts. He, slightly round and stout, dressed equally as bad, but on Sundays he would adorn a shiny brown pair of faux-leather loafers he was given in London. One shoe had a deep thin scratch across the toe that no amount of shoe polish could hide.

There was nothing remotely romantic between us. What we did come to eventually share was a growing hatred of Adegoke, my head of year and English teacher. If only we'd left the hatred where it began.

On my first day at senior school, I distinctly remember looking up from the ground at Adegoke as he stood at the front of our class. (Everyone called him Mr Adegoke, but privately, I'd long dropped the reverence of 'Mr') He was slim, quite beautiful, average height, with a low, perfectly rounded, jet-black Afro that sparkled in the sun – courtesy of Vaseline Hair Tonic, I'm sure. His safari suit was exquisitely ironed, and even the cloud of dust from the field couldn't hide the fact that his shoes were foreign and expensive. His smile was small but charismatic, his skin the colour of a perfectly tanned Nigerian Guinness head – unusual for a Yoruba man – and despite the heat, he seemed impervious to sweating. He exuded a quiet confidence and held the power of his position with ease and understatement. There were flickers of evidence in his accent that he had at some point or another lived in Europe or the States. I noted his fingers were devoid of jewellery. Unmarried. I felt flushed, imagining the crude way girls would tittle-tattle about him in fantasies one wouldn't expect of Nigerian teens from 'good homes.'

As he reassured my mother that I would be 'in safe hands at Mayflower Secondary' – one of Lagos State's semi-prestigious girls schools, I saw the way his eyes danced around her face and body. I saw the way she responded in kind. Both of them searching, both of them finding. It was as though I wasn't there. I looked down, burning with embarrassment, and for the millionth time in my life wished I had a normal mother.

Mama didn't act, look, or dress like other mothers who swaddled their middle-aged heft in *iro* and *buba* or spent their weekends in oversized tie-dye kaftans giving 'rich aunty vibes'. My mother was still young – in her late twenties – and so she wore fitted sleeveless tops, tight jeans, fancy heels. And whenever she wore traditional fabric, it was always sewn into fashionable Western styles: bustiers, fishtail skirts, one-shoulder dresses. So, of course, the mothers of my classmates always considered her with suspicion and snobbery; I was never invited to their houses.

My mother posed too much of a threat. Where other women had necks that thickened like cornstarch, my mother's remained lithe, minuscule, resistant to age. While they were married and worried about holding on to their philandering spouses, Mama was proudly free and footloose and couldn't care less that the town whispered about her promiscuity. She and her party-going friends – also single – were, without realizing it, running their own brand of feminism. They had no interest in being tied down to anyone. Including a child.

I've always said that if there was a rule book on what a mother was or should be, my mother had long discarded it. Her unorthodox way of existing, particularly as an African woman, made men – young, old, married, single, illiterate, seriously geriatric, whatever – want her more. Because don't we all want, crave, desire the thing that we cannot fully have?

I was still squirming at the realization that something was unfolding between my mother and Adegoke, when you walked by with your noisy gaggle of girlfriends one day. It was a welcome distraction. I noticed you immediately because, yes, you were beautiful, in the way that Nigerians automatically consider light-skinned, buxom females beautiful – but also because you were the only girl in the crowd who didn't have natural hair. Yours was relaxed. It made you seem more worldly. With your already rounded hips swaying as you passed by, I heard you laugh. A laugh that was big, full, and yet sophisticated. A laugh that showed off the gap between your two front teeth. A laugh that made your full chest rise dramatically. I realize now it was probably all for the benefit of Adegoke.

It was months later, outside the window of my shorthand class, when I first saw him talking to you. Now that I think about it, your indiscretion was stunning. You were holding an exercise book and a maths book, hugging them close. He was brushing (caressing?) something (invisible dirt?) from your collarbone. You looked sullen, and he looked like he was trying to appease you. The way he smiled. The way he coaxed. The way he touched you. The way your body language shifted in spite of itself. The way you melted. That's when I knew. Did you know that by then he was also already sleeping with my mother?

'Thin Line Between Love and Hate' by the Persuaders is

a song my mother would play on an old gramophone – a gift, like so much else, from a former beau, I imagine – in the house we shared with Alhaja. She played it over and over again, until the record was so scratched that when it got to the chorus, it would keep jumping. 'It's a thin line— It's a thin line— It's a thin line—' The more I think about Adegoke, the more that song comes back to me.

Adegoke was different from the many other men my mother had dalliances with. Men who embodied the heady con-coction of affluence and arrogance. They doused her with money and gifts and essentially financed her (our) life. Their reward – much to the chagrin of their ageing wives – was being able to show off my young beautiful mother at social events, like an awe-inspiring party trick. I balked at this but was also conflicted; I was well aware of how my school fees were paid. These men also saw nothing of putting wads of money in my small hands. 'Fine girl, take this, buy yourself something nice.' Even in my naivety, I knew that these men had amassed their wealth by fleecing the country through questionable business practices. I knew they probably had a wife (or two), another mistress (or two), and children (defi-nitely more than two) somewhere. People talked. My mother knew this, but she didn't care. She had no desire to topple their wives, understanding she held far more power by not belonging to one man. She played the game well: they used her; she used them. And when she got bored, or they became too needy (men had been known to show up unannounced, pleading with my grandmother to talk to her daughter to rekindle their romance), there would always be someone else waiting in the wings.

I had the lofty fantasy, one I have long held over all my mother's dalliances, that she would quickly move on from Adegoke and would suddenly, finally turn her affections, something I had never experienced, towards me. Considering her usual motivation was money, that my mother lingered much longer on Adegoke was a surprise. A shock, really. While there was apparently some family money, aside from the apartment in Ikoyi, which I'm sure his middle-class parents paid for, there were no glaring signs of great wealth. He didn't drive the latest Mercedes-Benz or Lexus. He didn't do the usual 'sugar daddy' thing of taking my mother to Federal Palace Hotel for the weekend. There was no gold watch or designer bag or shoes picked up for her on a business trip to Switzerland. No endless stacks of cash. Once, when Alhaja commented on the extreme ugliness of one particularly wealthy married lover, my mother responded tartly, 'It's not good looks that helped us to build this house.' When Adegoke started teaching my English literature classes, her preoccupation with him began to make sense. It didn't matter that he wasn't rich. It was his mind that was priceless. As with all Nigerian students, of course we studied Chinua Achebe. But Adegoke also introduced us to Oscar Wilde, Flaubert, Nabokov. I learned new words like 'nihilism' and 'profligacy', which were, of course, ridiculous, because who used them in normal conversation? But still, Adegoke was innately smart; he was cultured; he opened my mind and my eyes to a new way of seeing and thinking. The big-money men suddenly looked small and provincial in comparison.

I could see why you, my mother, and the other girls and women fell for him. Because I fell for him, too. Not that he noticed. And he didn't have to curry favour with me to have my mother's attention, so he treated me like any other student (well, except for you). I was nothing to him. Did you ever watch *Fatal Attraction*? There is a part where Glenn Close turns to Michael Douglas and says, 'I will not be ignored.' It was chilling to watch. But now, years on, I completely understand it. Because that's how I felt. Ignored. It was terrifying how quickly that emotion shifted my love and admiration for him into resentment. And then hate.

'It's a thin line—It's a thin line— It's a thin line—'

I hated the power he had over women, girls. Like me. Like you. Like my mother. How feminist of me, you might think. But no, I wasn't a feminist. I was jealous. My mother was drunk with Adegoke. Coquettish and giggly, her guard – especially unexpected, considering how she normally was with men – was embarrassingly down. She was forlorn and bad-tempered when he'd cancel their dates at the last minute or let her down in some way. She was so emotionally invested. She had given away her power. And then I saw Adegoke at school, spending all his time brushing the invisible dust off your shoulders. And all the time, I didn't exist.

My relationship with my mother has always been strange. It never mimicked the mother-daughter tropes I saw in films, negative or positive. I was an introvert. (Which is ironic, considering I now work in a job that is eternally social. But the superficiality of it means no one digs too deep so it's actually a great place to hide.) My mother, on the other hand, was the life of any party. She's the kind of woman whom you would imagine today would be dancing on TikTok with her daughter, and followers would incessantly comment, 'Wow, you guys look like sisters.' But there was no maternal instinct with my mother. I've often wondered whether this was because she had me so young. A child bringing up a child. Or having a doll. A doll that, every so often, you remember to pick up, play with and then discard because something or someone else has taken your fancy.

Still, since I hadn't seen her give any kind of real, meaningful commitment to any of her lovers, I slowly learned not to take it too personally. Adegoke changed that.

He sparked something in my mother I had never seen her give to anyone. Not any of the other men. And certainly not me. I hated him for it. I wanted to punish him for it. Which is why I sneaked a note in the headmistress's office about you and him sleeping together and threatened to go public with it. (Sorry, yes, that was me.) I discovered, much later on, that it was just one of the numerous claims of inappropriate behaviour that were levied against him that term. Mayflower Secondary covered it up until they couldn't afford to. He was quietly let go, as you know. And then his family contacts simply lined up another job for him. He became the headmaster at another girls school. A smaller school but a promotion, nonetheless. There's Nigeria for you. And he still continued to see my mother, because, of course, she swallowed his version of the story whole. Nothing had changed. And then it did.

One Saturday afternoon, Adegoke came to my grandmother's store to pick up my mother. I hid in the back; I'd become increasingly awkward around him – maybe he suspected I'd reported him? When they left, Bakare came to sit down at the bench in front of our shop as he always did. And I joined him. Since his deportation, he had been helping his grandmother sell mats, but business was slow. Because let's face it, who bought a new mat every day?

'You don't like him,' Bakare said pointedly, staring ahead as he stroked his imaginary beard.

I didn't answer. I twisted my hands and rubbed my feet against each other. He continued, taking my silence for agreement. 'I also don't like him. Just because he has been to London – have I not been? – and is now talking *fefefe* with his wide nose. He thinks he can come here and blow his grammar on us. Instead of him hiding his face in shame for carrying small, small schoolgirls up and down.' Surprise spread across my face, and he turned to me and laughed. 'Ah, ah, yes o, everybody knows.'

And this is how it started. Once he'd noticed my mother, dressed in her best lace, leave the shop with Adegoke, and Alhaja go inside to pray, like clockwork Bakare would come and sit on the bench. Our shared dislike of Adegoke opened up to me a side of Bakare I hadn't seen. He became so much more loquacious, sharing stories about his time in England. The cold – the climate and the people – the bad food, and the fact that the English always found an excuse for everything wrong with their people. In Nigeria, Bakare once argued, at least if someone commits a shocking crime like killing his neighbour, eating their flesh and burying the bones in his compound, they'd be labelled possessed and taken somewhere for 'deliverance' where the demons would be beaten out of him. 'In England they will say, "Poor chap, maybe he wasn't feeling in his right mind that day" – and so they put him in a place where he can eat three square meals a day, have visitors, play games, watch television...' According to

Bakare, that's what prison in the UK is like. He shook his head and laughed a tight, slightly brutal laugh, 'And yet they say Africans are mad.' He sounded so knowledgeable. I didn't ask him how he knew so much about the English incarceration system.

He became increasingly vocal in his disdain for Adegoke: he hated his voice, hated his laugh, and hated what he said was a 'prideful look. Like Lucifer'. There were moments of me feeling uneasy – I never truly understood exactly why Bakare hated Adegok – but still I'd laugh, relieved to finally be able to share my own hatred of my mother's lover. It was a conflicting feeling; I, like most everyone else, was still deeply drawn to him, his intelligence, his love of books. But I never defended him to Bakare. When Adegoke lent me his worn copy of John Steinbeck's *Of Mice and Men*, I struggled to hide my delight as I accepted it. Bakare, on the other hand, snorted disparagingly. '*Eh! Se na* book we go chop?!' and carelessly tipped out the filthy water his grandmother had just used to wash pots, soaking the toecaps of the expensive shoes worn by his nemesis. Both my mother and Adegoke were furious at the disrespect. Adegoke berated Bakare in a lofty mix of English and watered-down Yoruba. Both our grandmothers, on hearing the commotion, came out to placate the situation, forcing Bakare to offer a grovelling apology. Out of the adults' earshot, I agreed out loud – only Bakare heard – that Adegoke's reaction had been overblown. As he watched my mother leave with Adegoke, Bakare burned with embarrassment and a simmering anger. How that ended with Bakare and his boys – one of them, a corrupt police officer – deciding to teach Adegoke a grave lesson, I don't know.

The day the yellow bus crashed was the same morning I saw Bakare, dressed as he would be on a Sunday, like it was a special occasion. His boys arrived in an old, dark-coloured Volvo to pick him up. I heard his grandmother tell them to keep themselves out of trouble. '*E ma se wahala o.*' It was as if she knew. As he and his friends headed towards the car, Bakare turned and winked at me. I didn't see him for the rest of the day.

I don't really know what happened after that. No more than what everybody else knows. No more than what I read in *The Daily Times*: that a group of men in an old burgundy Volvo with a distorted registration plate ran Adegoke's car off the road. That Adegoke, losing control momentarily, swerved into the path of an oncoming yellow bus travelling in the opposite direction. That the yellow bus, full of passengers, crashed, its metal frame crunching against a band of trees. That the face-covered robbers, according to an unnamed survivor, were 'high on cannabis' and emptied passengers' pockets as they lay dying. That one of the robbers wore 'very shiny, brown leather-looking shoes' – one of which had a deep scratch across it that resembled 'the tail of a small lizard'.

After the accident, Bakare quietly left town. No one knew his whereabouts. My mother moved on to a new love interest; it turns out she wasn't as besotted with Adegoke as I thought. Or perhaps she was just not prepared to dedicate the rest of her life to a cripple. Just as she couldn't quite commit to a teenage daughter she never really grew to love. Of course, she would find this accusation offensive. I can imagine her retorting, 'Didn't I clothe you, send you to good schools, put food in your stomach?' She also paid for me to travel to London (initially to further my education,) but three weeks after my arrival, I caught the eye of a model scout, looking for an 'exotic' look. For a few years after I left Lagos, my mother and I put up the pretence of a relationship. But aside from the odd call and my flying back when Alhaja died, we barely speak. We'd both rather not be reminded of the past.

I ask myself whether it is my fault that Adegoke is now spending the rest of his life in a wheelchair. That so many people from the yellow bus died. What would have happened if I'd never spoken to Bakare? Could I have stopped this? And why am I writing this to you, a stranger, someone I barely knew? I'm not sure. Bu my therapist encouraged me to write and burn my letter after reading. I sometimes wonder what would have happened if I had given this to your gateman. I think of him often. The way he prayed so desperately, so fervently, for his soul. Recently, I've been tempted to join him and pray for mine.

ACKNOWLEDGEMENTS

Writing these stories, a process that began and stopped – and began and stopped – over a number of years, started as a way to indulge in 'What ifs'. I did this by writing stories that ultimately explore the way society, faith and culture shape – wrongly or rightly – women's lives. It was a solitary, private affair. Hence unlike most acknowledgements, you will see, unless you count me and God, I have no early draft readers. I finally found the courage to share it… I'd like to acknowledge the wonderful people who believed in me, believed in the stories and believed in the process to give birth to what you are now holding in your hands.

Pilar Queen, my incredible agent at UTA in New York. I am so greatly indebted to you. Your support and belief in me and these stories have been clear, extraordinary and single minded from the minute I (tentatively) shared them with you. (Did I ever tell you that I cried when you sent your unequivocally YES email?) Thank you, thank you, thank you.

Also, to Meredith Miller for everything you have done and for always having my back!

Adenike Olanrewaju at HarperCollins US. Where do I even begin? You are the editor of dreams. Your kindness, your brilliance, your sensitive but direct interrogation, your unshakeable support for me, your patience (!). Working with you, knowing you, has been an absolute balm, a gift that makes me feel so fortunate. The bar has been set very high...

To Juliet Mabey at Oneworld. What a privilege to have you as my UK editor and publisher. From the moment we met, I knew I wanted us to work together. Your energy and enthusiasm for this book has been nothing short of joyous – you are the ultimate cheerleader! I am grateful to you and the Oneworld team for having such an openness to my ideas, thoughts and direction. And for the meetings around the table at the Oneworld offices where great conversation, cake and cackling are always top of the agenda.

Special shout out to Liz Velez at HarperCollins. And the amazing design team. Your eye, your skills, your love of good typography and the swiftness in nailing Hermes Orange speaks to my heart in ways you cannot imagine.

Thank you to my family (you know who you all are!) for being understanding (well, most of the time!) when I couldn't always engage because, 'I just need to finish this book!'

Black women everywhere who, in big ways, in small ways, in everyday ways, challenge the box society tries to put you in, I salute you.

To God. My very first reader.

FUNMI FETTO is the Style Editor at British *Vogue* and has written for *The Sunday Times*, *Harper's Bazaar*, the *Telegraph*, *Elle*, and the *Guardian*. This is her first work of fiction.